The
Take

The Take

L. Brown

PRODIGY GOLD BOOKS

PHILADELPHIA   *   LOS ANGELES

THE TAKE

A Prodigy Gold Book

Prodigy Gold E-book edition/November 2017

Prodigy Gold Paperback edition/November 2017

Library of Congress Catalog Card Number: 2017944630

Website: http://www.prodigygoldbooks.com

Author's e-mail: lbrownthewriter@gmail.com

ISBN 978-1-939665-24-9

Published simultaneously in the US and Canada

PRINTED IN THE UNITED STATES OF AMERICA

For L'kia Nicole Brooks

(1979-1999)

ACKNOWLEDGEMENTS

If I were an island this page would be irrelevant, but as you (my esteemed readers) see, it's here, so let the praise commence.

My wonderful family, you came through for me in my darkest moment and blessed me with the mental wherewithal to get back to the light.

My editor, Locksie Locks, I call you "Mum" for your English heritage, but your support on a professional and personal level is infinitely nurturing. My literary siblings (Envy Red, Kristofer Clarke, Leonard Anderson, English Ruler, Pernitha Tinsley), you all dragged me into your lives and never let me go professionally or personally; you loved me in ways only family can and taught me the definition of friendship, proving I am not the wordsmith that I like to think I am considering I've been defining friend wrong my whole life.

It's odd to thank a barber, but I must thank Vergil Austin, as he has supported every novel that I've written; and, every time that I sit in his chair I always get up a tad wiser. Thanks for the words of wisdom.

Devone "Reds" Johnson, thanks for the inside job, bro. One day we'll laugh about allowing me to use your...well, it wouldn't be an inside job if I exposed it here. Frankie "ChukTizzy" Taylor you read these words when they were chicken scratch in a notebook and want to play, Naim Butler, in the movie adaptation. Thanks for dragging me to the gym to work out to clear my head. I'm down thirty pounds and feeling good because of your help, persistence, and dedication to my physique goals. Jermaine Coleman, Perry Williams, Kaseem Clark, Lamont Fleming, Tye Davis, Juma Sampson, Aree Toulson thanks for helping me shape my main character into the man that he is.

Kisha Green, what a way to pick me up by answering all of my questions along the way to completing this project; thank you, again.

As I wrote this novel, I taught a literary workshop to some men in prison, The Fort Dix Six: Sage, Craig P, Six Pack, Rob, Woo, and H. Helping you, helped me, as every class that I prepared for you, I learned a lesson of my own while researching. You will all be grand authors one day soon.

Lastly, I must thank my initial critiquers and reviewers. I needed your fierce feedback. I laughed, I kicked, I screamed, I grew, and now the readers are blessed.

The
Take

PROLOGUE

"Everybody! Get down on the ground!" Feeq blurted as he and Reem moved swiftly from the vestibule into the lobby of the brick and mortar bank.

The frantic bank employees and customers were froze in shock when the two masked men entered the bank with weapons drawn and pointed, making threatening demands for everyone to get down on the floor with their hands in sight.

They complied.

"Think about your lives. Think about your families. Stay down, and you'll make it home to see them another night. We're here for the bank's money. This will be over in a matter of minutes," Reem stated calmly.

They moved quickly to gain control of the occupants of the old-fashioned bank. Reem towered over the innocent victims, incessantly instructing them to remain on the floor, facedown. He felt in control and powerful as his adrenaline started to rush.

Feeq vaulted over the teller's station like an Olympic superstar clearing hurdles in a two hundred meter dash. The two tellers were already lying, flat faced, on the floor. One was a young black male; the other a middle-aged white woman. The dude was no more than thirty years old. He was trembling and what sounded like sobbing was coming from his direction in muffled sniffles.

Feeq told the tellers to get up from the floor and open the drawers and tellers' safes. To his surprise, the male teller didn't budge. He remained on the floor, and Feeq was now sure he was crying because he was shaking with revulsion. For a second, Feeq nearly snapped on him, but he decided to let him be.

After raising the large .45 Smith and Wesson to the female teller's face, Feeq demanded, "Open the drawers and safes! No dye-packs, no bait-bills, and no fucking alarms!"

Her eyes were the size of half-dollars. She cringed as she peered through her thin, wire-framed glasses, down the barrel of death. It was hard for her fog-filled mind to register the blabber coming from the uncovered mouth behind the dark mask. Common sense told her to open the drawers and safes, so she did.

After opening them, she took a step back. Without being told to, she dropped back down and sank her face into the carpet. Feeq, floundering with the stacks of bills, quickly stuffed the gym bag.

He leaped back over the station and into the lobby.

"Where's the manager?" he shouted to the frightened group lying on the open floor.

A middle-aged white woman rose to her knees, as Feeq slid the bag filled with money toward Reem. He was sitting at one of the desks on the open floor and observing the victims. Feeq caught the empty bag Reem threw back to him in mid-air.

"Are you the manager?" Feeq asked the woman after the bag exchange.

She nodded and began to say something, but, before she could utter a word, he grasped a handful of her shoulder-length blond hair. She shrieked from the pain and succumbed to his authority.

Her frail body flew across the lobby. She was attempting to keep up with her hair as he violently dragged her by it across the bank. She was sure that she knew where he was taking her. Actually, she was as anxious as him to get there, so that it could all be over with.

The manager twirled the nozzle on the vault's lock several times. Thoughts of her family were glued in her head: Kevin, Katie, and Damon—her son, daughter, and husband. *Will I ever see them again? Are they safe?* She nearly broke from the fear of the thought of never seeing them again.

Her violent quaking interfered with her ability to concentrate, so she spun the lock's nozzle past its correct numbers several times. Feeq was excited and was doing a little trembling of his own.

"Relax," he calmly told her. "No one is going to get hurt. This will all be over in a few seconds. Now take your time and open the vault."

"Okay. Just don't hurt anyone, please," she pleaded.

"Do you have kids?" he asked her. She nodded. "Think about your kids."

That's exactly what I've been doing, she thought sarcastically. Finally, there was a series of clicks followed

3

by a hydraulic hiss of air. The vault's door slowly swung open. Feeq's eyes widened, filling the capacity of the holes in the ski mask he donned. For a moment, maybe two, he was paralyzed by the sight of the stacks of dead presidents. Benjee stared at him.

One corner of his mouth curved upward, forming a crooked, toothless grin as he looked at his reward. The manager let out a sigh of relief. Her reward felt even greater—at least, to her anyway. He had finally let go of her hair.

CHAPTER 1

Dark clouds imprisoned the sun and stripped the morning brightness from the sky. Darkness invaded the ceiling of the city of Philly. Rain fell from the steel curtain, pouring over the windshield of the stolen Dodge Caravan.

Sitting behind the wheel of the stolen van, Donnie spoke into the Boost mobile phone, using the phone's chirp feature.

"Yo! Y'all have been in there over three minutes," he said to Reem through the airwaves. "I'm pulling up out front right now. Let's go!" He snapped the phone closed after a chattered response from Reem on the other end.

Moments later, just as Donnie pulled the van into the plaza's parking lot, Reem and Feeq exited the double doors of the bank. They were outside the PNC Bank, at the northeast exit. The branch was a freestanding bank with a drive-through lane. It was surrounded by big-box retail stores: Walmart, Best Buy, Home Depot, and Burlington Coat Factory.

5

None of the early morning commuters noticed them as they trotted toward the dented, navy-blue minivan. Donnie wore a devilish grin on his face as he watched his boys approach with bags of money. They hopped in. Feeq was in the passenger seat, and Reem was in the rear passenger compartment. The van skidded into motion before they managed to shut their doors. They ripped their masks off once they were out the scope of the overhead cameras.

"We fucking did it!" Reem shouted excitedly from the back of the van.

They all shouted and celebrated, sharing the same exalted feeling. The excitement and adrenaline could be felt. It traveled through the van like a current.

They cruised at a normal pace, stopping at all lights for the next several minutes to blend in with traffic. Getting to the next point undetected was crucial, so they could switch cars before the van became hot. The getaway was a stealthy procedure, so they had to attract little attention.

In the distance up ahead, red and blue-bubbled lights illuminated the streets. The deafening sirens hollered angrily as the police cars scurried up the wet tarmac.

"Sit back, y'all. Sit back!" Donnie panicked.

Feeq and Donnie sat up straight in their seats up front, while Reem lay stretched across the rear seat. He stared down at the bags containing the money and wondered how much they were getting away with.

Donnie gripped the steering wheel with both hands perspiring from being inside the leather gloves. Two police cars raced past them without so much as a head turn. Donnie made a sharp right turn, and the screaming sirens became faint. He drove another half block before whipping into a deserted driveway, reaching the switch point.

They hurried out the van but tried to appear as calm and normal as possible. Reem carried the two stuffed bags to the switch car. Feeq jumped in the driver's seat of a taupe-grey Ford Expedition. The other two climbed in and laid in the back to make it appear like Feeq was the truck's sole occupant. Then, they disappeared into traffic.

Once they arrived at home, they dumped the bags on the floor. Donnie and Reem's eyes were the size of quarters at the sight of the mountain of money. Although this was their first time committing a bank robbery, Feeq remained nonchalant. The thirty-one-year-old had six years on the other two. He shared in their excitement, but he was doing a good job disguising it.

Feeq had been at this financial stage before. Years ago, he had run several coke houses, which moved a few ounces a day. Not a lot, but a few ounces a day started to add up when he accumulated his money. But, since what goes up must come down and after being shot five times in a botched robbery of some Jamaicans, Feeq had never bounced back until then.

Feeq sat on the cracked black leather couch, rolling some weed in a Dutch. They were in the basement of Reem's grandmother's house. If she had been aware of what they were up to in the basement, she would've had a fit. They'd have to break Grams off a nice check—even then; they'd never hear the end of her mouth. Grams wouldn't call the cops, though. She was old school, and calling the cops wasn't her forte, but getting a check was.

Reem looked at Feeq and noticed that the Dutch was half gone.

"Yo! Pass the fucking weed, man!" he snapped with a smirk on his face.

"Roll some more Dutches up," Donnie told Feeq.

"What the fuck I look like? Cousin E?" he responded.

They all shared a laugh, but Feeq reached in his pocket hanging on the armrest of the couch and grabbed some more Dutches.

While Feeq rolled the weed, Reem and Donnie were crouched on the floor, separating the money and getting rid of all the bank's wrappers that banded the stacks of bills. From the looks of things, they estimated that they had come up, at least, a hundred thousand. Not bad for the first take.

Reem took a long drag of the Dutch and aspirated, "Yo! Count it out in stacks of thousands and put them to the side." He spoke in a pursy tone, trying to hold the weed smoke in.

"Twenty-forty-sixty-eighty-hundred," Donnie counted a stack of twenties out loud.

"Man, you're going to be all damn day counting that shit like that!" Feeq snapped on Donnie, who was his nephew. "Fifty twenties is a stack, so count them out like that!"

"We already got a bunch of them over here that had the wrappers with the amounts on them, so they don't need to be counted," Reem said.

As Feeq looked at the money, a grin finally surfaced on his face. "Y'all little niggas ain't gonna know how to act now that y'all got a little paper."

"We been getting money," Donnie said.

"Please, you don't even know how to count the paper, talking 'bout you been getting it." Feeq shook his head, continuing to clown his nephew.

Reem took another puff of the weed. "We're going to the auction and shopping tomorrow."

"See what I mean?" Feeq responded flatly, shaking his head again.

"We're gonna get some more work, too." Donnie looked at Reem. "Flood the block," he added with excitement.

"Yeah, this is just the beginning," Reem agreed, looking at his right-hand man with a Broadway smile spread across his face. "Your new nickname is Donnie Schemes."

Inside the dull white holding cell, located inside the Curran-Fromhold Correctional Facility, Kevin "Ghost" Rines was growing more and more impatient. He was moments away from being released from CFCF. The female guard stationed behind the off-white tile counter was typing on the prison's computer. She had noticed Ghost's impatience. She had observed him neglect the ridged-steel benches. Instead, he was pacing back and forth inside the eight by ten cage.

Periodically, he'd pause at the locked sliding door and glare through the thick Plexiglas with a cold stare in his dark brown eyes. His almond-shaped eyes revealed more than the anxiousness and excitement of someone being released back into society.

Ghost, who was five feet nine inches, had a scrawny frame. He weighed no more than 150 pounds. At twenty-six, his light complexion and light facial hair gave him a baby face. He still could pass for twenty, maybe twenty-one. If looks could kill, he wouldn't be doing any murdering.

But his eyes were his most intimidating feature. Along with the constant screw face, his eyes beamed corruption. Beyond them was a young man bearing lots of pain. The look he gave the female correctional officer made her uneasy, so she kept her gaze fixed on the computer screen.

"Lazy bitch is probably on that Facebook or Twitter shit," Ghost mumbled to himself. "She needs to get me the fuck outta here."

Unfortunately, it wasn't her call to let him out. They both were waiting for the chubby sergeant to come and complete the standard release procedure, which included a bunch of biological questions like name, D.O.B., address, social security number, and all that bullshit, to make sure they weren't releasing the wrong person. Despite all that, they still let the wrong people go all the time.

Ghost finally took a seat on the cold bench and leaned his head against the cement block wall behind him. Although he was only down for six months, the skid bid had felt like six years spent in the manmade fortress. Tucking his arms inside his blue prison shirt to escape the frigid, ventilated air, he let out a deep sigh and drifted off, recalling the memories that had placed him in this box to begin with.

June 2nd

"Damn, Ghost! You're high as shit," Donnie told Ghost as he looked at his dumbfounded facial expression.

"I ain't even feeling it like that," he responded with a slur.

A few hours ago, Ghost had dumped eight Xanax and sipped an ounce of purple syrup containing Phenergan and Codeine. For some reason, when taking xanies and syrup, people always appeared higher to others than they actually felt.

That was the exact case with Ghost on this particular evening. He was dumb-high, but felt that everything was normal and that he was sober. However, he was far from it. If Lindell, the crack head who ran the pill spot, hadn't run out of xanies, he'd have had more than the eight already circulating through his system.

Ghost, Donnie, and Reem, along with several stragglers, stood on the block, grinding. It was another typical evening on Boyer and Locust Streets. The sun was just past setting. The orange lining illuminating the skyline was visible as the sun crept below the horizon. The late spring air created a warm breeze.

More stragglers were in the liter-infested alleyway, shooting dice. There was a rush on the block, so Ghost and his boys weren't attending to the overcrowded crap game. Instead, they were serving the fiends scrambling up and down the two one-way streets that intersected where they stood.

They took turns serving the fiends to keep things organized, rather than racing up to crack heads on some scrambling shit. Most of the time, they'd serve fiends in sync. They all maintained their own personal clientele that only they served unless they weren't out there at the time when the others could serve them.

"Yo! What's good? Y'all wanna hit Onyx tonight?" Reem asked. "Y'all know it's Two Dollar Tuesday tonight."

"Yeah, I'm sliding down there later on. I know the bitches are gonna be out tonight," Donnie responded. "You going down there, Ghost?"

"Naw, you know I don't do the strip club like that. Wifey would have a fit."

"Pussy-whipped-ass nigga!" Reem commented, and he and Donnie shared a chuckle.

Ghost didn't find the remark amusing.

"Whatever!" he snapped with an angry slur.

"Nigga, you on an emotional roller coaster. Get outta ya feelings," Reem said with a dismissive hand wave.

"What?"

The two of them went through these types of arguments all the time. Sometimes, the arguments lasted for hours at a time. This was one of those instances, but Donnie interrupted them.

"Yo! Is that Reese up there, talking to Aunt Lisa?" he said, using his chin to point up the street in Reese's direction.

Aunt Lisa was a local fiend and one of the best customers in the hood. She owned a rundown red brick on Sprague Street. Looking straight down Locust Avenue, one could see where the two blocks met.

Lisa could run traffic like a Manhattan rush hour, keeping the crumbled bills pouring in. Her two-story brick hole stayed packed with reeking smokers, chasing the feeling of their first hit.

They never found it.

Reem and Ghost stopped their petty arguing and turned their heads as they gazed up the street.

"Yeah, that's that nigga," Reem said, biting his lip.

Reem and Donnie were already treading up the sidewalk before Ghost could move an inch. Just days before, Ghost and Reem had had a heated argument with Reese about cut-throating. Reese thought, because Lindell was his mom, he could stand out on Locust Street, hustling, but Ghost and his goons weren't going for that.

Reese would disrespectfully stand at the top of Locust and persuade smokers to cop off him, rather than them. Most fiends remained loyal to not only Ghost and them, but the better work, while others opted not to walk the stretch. So, they'd buy off Reese instead.

Reese observed them, heading in his direction, and could tell, by their demeanors, that they were heated.

"Here we go again," he mumbled to himself.

"Yo! Didn't we tell you a couple of days ago to stay off the block!" Reem snapped. It was more of a statement than a question.

"I know, Reem, but, shit, it's enough paper out here for all of us to eat. Plus, it's the first of the month," he pled, hoping they'd understand. "She only wanted five for $40 anyway."

Aunt Lisa was gone. She had peeped the twisted-faced men heading up the block and hastily stuck the bags in her mouth. Then, she took off with her famous speed racer bop. She knew she'd hear about her copping off someone else later, but, shit, money was money, so it wasn't like they would stop serving her.

"Besides, she said the trick at her house wanted my shit anyway," Reese blurted arrogantly.

"Look out, Reem!" Ghost said, slightly shoving Reem to the side with his arm stretched out. The glare of the shiny, chrome 9mm clasped in Ghost's hand caught the attention of Reese, and he reluctantly stepped back.

"What? You gonna shoot me, you bitch ass?"

The haughty words coming out of Reese's mouth were cut short by the thumping strike of the pistol against his furrowed eyebrow. He let out a squeal as he abruptly crashed to the ground. Blood gushed from a gash over his brow, covering the pavement with a crimson puddle.

"Didn't I tell you..."

Cluck! Another vicious blow and the sound of metal against flesh, while Ghost snapped.

"Not to come back around..."

Cluck!

"Here again?" Ghost exclaimed viciously.

There was a roaring echo throughout the block. The impact from the last strike had made the gun explode. Ghost ignored the sound and started kicking the balled-up figure on the ground.

Ghost wore a devilish grin, and beads of sweat escaped his glands as they trickled down his face. He had zoned out, like a mad man. Reem and Donnie both stood there, watching motionlessly like they were suffering from paresis. Ghost was usually humble, but hotheaded. Once ticked off, this was usually the outcome.

Ghost stood straight up, aimed the weapon at Reese's defenseless body and fired a shot.

Pow! The sound echoed off the brick row homes and traveled down the street.

"Ah, ah, ah!" Reese screamed from the excruciating pain the bullet sent through his body.

"Please don't kill me!" Reese pleaded openly for his life, waving his hands in front of his face.

"Ghost! Don't hurt my baby!" Lindell, who had heard the shots, shouted and headed toward the corner. Ghost ignored her and her son's pleas.

Pow! Pow! Two more explosions ripped through before there were a few clicking sounds. The slide of the gun had stuck in position, as if the gun was de-cocked. Ghost pulled the trigger several more times, but there was a series of rebellious clicks. The gun jammed on him.

If it hadn't, Reese would have been a dead man.

CHAPTER 2

Ghost was snapped out of the reverie by a noisy sound. He opened his eyes to find the chubby sergeant tapping his keys against the Plexiglas and guessed that was his cue to roll.

The release process took a mere five minutes after a tedious ninety-minute wait inside the holding cell of the receiving and discharge department.

All of that was behind him now—nothing more than a memory. He was now taking the "walk of fame," a term used by inmates when someone was being let out of the concrete jungle.

Once outside, Ghost took a deep breath, giving his lungs a taste of fresh air. The air smelled and felt fresher. Smelled like freedom—whatever that smelled like. It was better than the ventilated air circulating throughout the rusty HVAC system installed on the other side of the walls.

Despite the late fall weather, the temperature was well in the mid-fifties. Not bad for an early morning in November. The sky was partly cloudy. You could see the sun wrestling to burst through the stingy clouds.

With the drugs out of his system and the established eating intake, Ghost's skin was glowing. It was a bit paler than usual from the lack of sun, but the sun's rays would tone it in no time. Whoever said prison preserved a person wasn't lying. Ghost's jet-black hair was shining from the African Pride hair grease. It complemented the deep waves circulating his head.

Kia, Ghost's girl, sat behind the wheel of the Park Avenue. It was the same car he had obtained the pistol from on the day he had crushed and nearly killed Reese. The vehicle was glossy beige with a cream ragtop.

He could make out her figure through the twenty percent tint slapped on the windows.

"There goes my *baaaby!*" he crooned, quoting the Usher song, which had come blasting through his earbuds on countless nights. Kia, doing some singing of her own, was bobbing her head in the car and had not yet seen him approaching.

Finally, she turned her head and saw her king heading toward the car. Butterflies flew through her curvaceous frame, giving her the heebie-jeebies. A rapid shudder shot through her body like she had been tased. After four years of being together, he still gave her that amazing feeling.

She hopped out the car and ran into his warm embrace. The bosom was tight as he clutched her in his arms. He felt like he never wanted to let her go again. They shared a long, intimate kiss, and he buried his face in her neck. He could smell the luscious fragrance vaporizing from her. He couldn't place the scent, but it was familiar, something from her massive collection.

Ghost and Kia had two different body shapes, but were roughly the same weight. However, her 150 pounds were crammed in a five foot five figure. Her skin was tawny. Her jet-black hair fell over her right shoulder, resting on her breast.

"Hey, baby. Look at you," he said as he slid his hands from her shoulders and down her arms, taking her hands into his.

She blushed and smiled, revealing perfect teeth.

"Stop, boy!" she said, slapping his arm. "You got me all blushing and shit."

Her looks were what had initially attracted him to her several years ago. She put men in a state of awe on her worst days. However, over the years, Ghost learned to really appreciate her for more than just her physical appearance. She was an ambitious individual, who had goals, and the number one characteristic she possessed was loyalty.

She had demonstrated her loyalty extensively over the last few months. She was always one of the first visitors at the jail on scheduled visiting days. She accepted every call, anticipating his calls more than he anticipated calling home. That was a lot of anticipation, to be more anxious than someone calling his wife from jail. She flooded him with mail: letters, cards, poems, and photo album-filling amounts of flicks.

"You been in there working out?" she asked with a seductive facial expression as she felt on his chest and arms.

"Girl, you gonna molest me out here?" he joked. "I'll take you right here on top of this car if you keep playing."

"Umm, let's go," she joked back.

Ghost was wearing standard prison clothes and was dying to get out of them. Navy blue khakis lazily drooped over some classic black and white Chuck Taylors. An off-white thermal top hugged his frame, revealing his toned upper body.

As they were getting in the car, two female visitors were strutting pass, toward the institution's entrance. Ghost could hear loud clanking sounds vibrating from the rectangular window above. The banging clamored through the facility's parking lot.

The sound was a louder version of a woodpecker beating at the back of a tree. Ghost was instantly familiar with the noise. It was the inmates trapped on the other side of the window banging on them with their brushes. They were seeking the attention of the women walking by in hopes of getting a peep show. Occasionally, a rider would walk by and flash them. Ghost knew firsthand because, less than twenty-four hours ago, he had been on the other side with his brush in his hand.

The ride home took close to half an hour. During his downtime, Ghost and Kia had agreed that he'd move in with her and her son. She didn't want Ghost back at the brick house that he and Donnie rented from a smoker.

Kia had a nice, little spot out in the purlieu of Philly in a section called Manayunk. There, he could escape the madness of

the hood and spend time with wifey and her six-year-old son, Khashan.

After riding by several fast-food joints, Ghost was starving, so he said, "Let's stop and get something to eat, baby."

"Boy, now you know I'm gonna make you something to eat," she responded. "Plus, I need some of that dick." She reached and planted her hand in his lap. "You kept me waiting long enough," she said, continuing to grope his manhood. "And I hope you know you're spending the whole day with me. I know you want to see your friends, but they're gonna have to wait. I wish you would leave those nothing-ass niggas alone anyway."

"Here we go again."

"I know we've been through this a million times, but I don't know what it will take for you to see who really cares about you. Besides Donnie, the rest of them don't give a shit about you, Ghost!" She pouted, after speaking truthful words.

But Ghost never listened.

"I know, baby." He leaned over the center console and kissed her on the cheek, trying to defuse the situation. "I'm gonna get my shit together this time around."

She glanced at him with an unsure look. It wasn't the first time she'd heard the promises about how he was a changed man and how he would get his life together; she really hoped his words were sincere this time because she couldn't stand another heartbreak.

"You still didn't say you were gonna spend the day with me!" she snapped. "And Kha's really looking forward to seeing you when he gets home from school this afternoon."

"Babe, come on. It goes without saying."

There was a moment of silence for the next several minutes. Kia's words were sinking in his head like a favorite song. They went in one ear, but didn't make it out the other as he thought about how things could have been worse. If it wasn't for the cheap-ass Bryco nine-millimeter jamming, Reese would have been a corpse and locked up with a life-sentence.

Donnie was the only one of his homies who had held him down. The others had abandoned him, neglecting to send money or even a letter. All of this weighed heavily on his mind. He had goals, and he really wanted to leave the game alone. It was never that simple, but living outside the hood was a start.

Silence was broken once they arrived in front of the luxury apartments. They had silently agreed to drop the subject because neither mentioned another word about it.

As soon as the front door cracked, the intimacy began. They were all over each other like it was their first time having sex together. She threw her arms around his neck, and he invited the embrace. He cupped her ass cheeks in his hands, and they kissed passionately. The front door creaked closed as they maneuvered inside the living room.

Kia put one hand on his chest, shoving him onto the cream leather couch. He submitted to her aggressiveness and let her take control. She slowly slid her index finger up his lips.

She hushed him and demanded, "Don't move."

He watched with lustful eyes as she disappeared down the hallway. He couldn't help but wonder what she was up to as he stripped out of his clothes. *She didn't mean don't move literally, did she?* Moments later, she ap-

peared back in the living room, undressed, but conceal-
ing her beauty under a pink bathrobe. The robe wasn't
much help because her dynamic curves were busting
through the lining.

She peeped that he was stripped down to his boxers. "Didn't I tell you not to move?"

"I know."

"Shhh." His sentence was cut off by that powerful
finger again. Once again, she pushed it up against his
mouth. She took him by the hand and pulled him from
the couch down the hallway. Her aggressiveness was
turning him on; she glanced down at his dick, bulging
out his boxers, and took it into her hand, gently pulling
him by his shaft into the bathroom.

The water in the bathtub was running, creating a
cloud of steam. The moisture in the air was soothing
against their skin.

"Drop 'em!" she demanded with authority.

He was used to those words from prison guards,
but those words, coming from his girl, were mind-blowing. He'd never heard her talk like this, but he was definitely digging it.

"Yes, ma'am," he said, playing along, as he stepped
out of his boxers.

"Now, step in and take a seat."

He lowered himself into the bubble-filled tub. He
couldn't help but think he was supposed to be the one
doing this for her. This was definitely different.

She untied the bow and let the robe swivel down
her body into a pile around her beautiful feet. She had
on a sexy two-piece lingerie set. The two pieces were
see-through, so Ghost stared in awe. Her body resembled the curvy vixens he had looked at in magazines

over the last several months: 36D chest, twenty-six-inch waist with a little-to-no fat hugging her abdomen, and a nice ass.

She seductively removed the lingerie one piece at a time. He stared at her, looking up and down, from her hazelnut eyes to her precious little feet. She bent over the tub and washed him with a lathered loofah.

Finally, she stepped into the tub with him. He was memorized by the effect she was having on him. Her body disappeared under the foamy bubbles stationed above the water as she lowered herself into it.

After a period of washing, kissing, and massaging, they made their way to the bedroom.

Ghost was startled when she opened the bedroom door. The shades were drawn closed to block the sunlight. Several candles were burning, dimly lighting the room. The entire room was resplendent. The floor and bed were mottled with various colored rose petals. The air was filled with a vanilla almond aroma. The mood was relaxed, and things were just right.

He was shocked by her creativeness. She snatched a remote from the dresser and aimed it at the Bose stereo system. Trey Songz's, *Love Faces*, came soothing through the speakers.

Oh, she definitely put this together, he thought as she backed to the edge of the bed and slowly laid down. It was obvious that she now wanted him to take control, so he did. He inched toward her and caressed her feet. He lightly ran his fingers along her body, as if he were strumming a guitar. Her body fluttered from the sensual touching.

He lay on top of her, passionately nibbling on her neck and earlobes. He let his fingers swim through her strands of hair. She let out a series of moans and cries.

"Please," she said, begging him to go inside her.

He was so hard it hurt. Her walls were tight as he entered her in the missionary position. She shrieked from the pain, but her pain quickly transformed into pleasure.

He thrust in and out of her as far as his pelvic bone would allow. Their bodies moved in rhythm to the music, and they both made the love faces Trey was referring to. Perspiration escaped their bodies as the lovemaking heated up.

Kia blurted out more cries. Her pelvic muscles tightened, and she forcefully raised her hips, reaching her climax. She sunk her nails into his back, grinding them into his skin.

"I love you, baby," she purred.

"I love you, too," he responded in a broken whisper.

He let out several moans of his own as he reached his peak. He picked up the speed of his thrusts, chasing the best feeling known to man.

"Cum in me; cum in me," she enticingly whispered in his ear. She wrapped her legs around his waist, clutching tightly just as he released in her.

He quivered, then collapsed on top of her. The two of them were breathing profoundly. They lost time of how long they laid there, cuddling. Eventually, she climbed out the bed, leaving him lying there, spread-eagle.

"Just like I promised, I'm about to make you something to eat."

He nodded and watched his baby in amazement. He was at a loss for words. Besides the slippers she slipped into, she left the room completely naked. He laid there in a trance.

He was home, he'd just had some of the best sex of his life, and now his wife was in the kitchen, butt naked and cooking.

Damn! Life is good.

CHAPTER 3

The following day, Donnie and Ghost linked up in uptown. Ghost parked the Buick Park Avenue and hopped in with Donnie in a jet-black Mercury.

The tint on the windows was as dark as the car's door panels, making it impossible to see inside.

"Here," Donnie said, handing Ghost a stack of bills as soon as he got in the car. Ghost took the bills without hesitation and started counting the bread, which totaled two thousand. Not much, but anything was helpful.

"Good looking. I needed this. I have to get back." Ghost showed his gratitude. "So, what you doing out here?" He asked. He was curious about how his man was getting to a dollar.

Donnie filled him in on a bank robbery they had committed several days ago. Ghost listened intently as Donnie boasted about the events. The lump sum they received caught Ghost's attention immediately.

They'd gotten away with $142,000, and Ghost was thinking about what he could do with a nice piece of paper like that right then. Although they had a little block and a crack house, they had never had that much change at once. Potentially they could have, but they loved to splurge—or do what they thought was splurging.

Up until this point, they'd been petty hustlers, but they'd just graduated from committing petty crimes to doing federal offenses that they could get crushed for.

Ghost knew, if he committed a robbery, he would have to invest his money in something legit to keep his promise to Kia about getting out of the game before it was too late.

Donnie made things sound so sweet, like it was no way for them to get caught. He was trying to persuade Ghost to take something down with him. Though Ghost had yet to utter a word back, he was already counting his money in his head.

"So you have another bank in mind?" Ghost asked, finally showing interest.

"Ain't no question."

"I thought you would never ask," Donnie said, smiling ear to ear. He knew his boy was down for whatever.

Donnie reached into the center console and said, "Here. Take a sip." He handed Ghost half a bottle of Henny.

Just as they were about to pull off, a car cruised up the block. A silver Ford Crown Victoria with tinted windows came to a halt next to them and blocked them in their parking spot. Ghost reached for the gun that was tucked in his waistband, but Donnie stretched his arm out, stopping him.

"Chill. That's Reem."

The driver's window inched down, revealing Reem behind the wheel. A cloud of smoke wreathed into the air with the strong odor of weed following it.

"Oh, shit! When you get home, nigga?" Reem asked, after realizing Ghost was in the passenger seat.

"Yesterday," Ghost responded, but he lacked the same enthusiasm in his voice.

"Yo! My bad! I didn't get at you while you were down. I saw your girl and asked her did you need anything, but she said you were good," he said, trying to make an excuse for his disloyalty.

"Yeah," Ghost responded dryly. He glanced at him with a cold stare in his eyes. He wasn't trying to hear the bullshit Reem was kicking. *Reem didn't get at me one time while I was down, and now he's trying to justify that shit? Unbelievable.*

The three of them had grown up together; they'd known one another since snotty noses in elementary school. From then until now, they'd hung together on a daily basis. They had shared countless memories together.

It really hurt Ghost that Reem didn't take the initiative to get at him once. It was bigger than money—though a check would have been nice—but a letter just to show concern was the least he could do. Or maybe he wasn't worth his time.

Up until now, Ghost felt like they were airtight and loyal to one another. To him, without loyalty, instead of a friend, he had a complete stranger in his circle. Reem now looked unfamiliar.

Reem leaned out the window and yelled, "Donnie Schemes! What's good, nigga?"

He quickly brushed Ghost's attitude off by diverting his attention toward Donnie.

Donnie was feeling the new nickname Schemes. He had received the name after putting together the scheme to rob the PNC bank. He had put the entire plan together: the casing of the bank, the stolen minivan, the switch point—all a vision he had mapped out to be perfectly executed.

He was digging himself. He turned his swag up on a million, emphasized the bop in his walk, and gestured like a ball player. At six foot, he kept a fitted cap pulled down to his brows. His beard stayed smothered with grease, and he was a slick talker. He could talk his way out of anything and others, into whatever he desired. Like he had just talked Ghost into taking something down.

"What's good, Reem? We're about to go look at another bank."

Ghost grimaced. He didn't necessarily agree with Donnie telling Reem the plan. Though they were childhood friends, he still had some animosity toward him for neglecting him while he was down.

"That's what I'm talking about, baby! You heard what Kiss said, 'Nowadays they given Rico out to the gang leader, to tell the truth dawg to hit a bank sweeter!'" Reem said excitedly, trying to quote Jadakiss's lyrics. "Yo, I'm going to hop in there with y'all." He pulled off wildly, whipping the car into a vacant parking spot.

After jumping in the car with Donnie and Ghost, the three of them drove to the bank to do some homework. For several minutes, they rode in silence. The music played low, and the mood in the car was sort of morbid. The three of them were obviously in deep thought, tuning out the music.

Reem broke the silence, saying, "Here."

He stretched a stack of bills over the seat and over Ghost's shoulder. Maybe breaking his man off a check would alleviate his thoughts about his disloyalty.

"It's a stack," Reem told him. "I'll hit you again, but that's what I got on me right now."

Ghost reluctantly took the change and stuffed it in his pocket. He knew the guilt was as heavy on Reem's chest as the heat that was coming off of his. The look on Reem's face had been discernible from the moment he saw Ghost sitting in the car. They both knew Ghost needed the money. And what better way to make things right than to pass off a couple dollars?

"I really feel some type of way about you not getting at me," Ghost finally said, tired of suppressing his emotions.

Reem cut off the long-winded lecture and rambling Ghost was getting ready to start.

"My bad, nigga," he said sincerely. "I was caught up out here, and I realize how you feel. It's no excuse, so I ain't even tryna justify it. I was outta line, and that shit won't happen again, homie."

Ghost felt the apology was sincere, but he wasn't going to drop it that easily. "Man, we've held each other down since snotty noses in the playground and playing manhunt."

The talk lasted ten minutes into the ride, but the silence overpowered and lasted the rest of the ride. They all lingered over the talk and heartfelt words. They knew the tension would die, but time had to do its job. They always fought, fell out, and disagreed, but they would always eventually return to being the brothers they were.

Donnie could make out the bank up ahead. They traveled up Germantown Avenue, crossing into the Chestnut Hill section of Philadelphia.

"There it goes. Right there," Donnie whispered as if someone outside the car could hear him.

"This jawn look sweet!" Reem snapped in excitement.

They all glanced at the Sovereign Bank, which was a rather small branch of the big-time bank. It was a standalone bank, resting on the corner. They crept by, attempting to be inconspicuous. There was a bus terminal directly across the street, flowing with commuters. On the other side of the ave, there was a train station, also, pouring with early-goers. A newsstand was obscuring the view of stragglers standing above the platform from seeing the bank—perfect.

They bent the block to get another look at things. Ghost took note of the front and side entrances. The decorative bushes in front of the bank blocked part of the front window.

The side entrance stood out because it was adjacent to a walkway that was between the bank and a little no-name store. The walkway led to a parking lot behind the bank. There was another driveway leading to a small block from the parking lot. It was the perfect getaway route. Almost as if the bank was set up to be taken down.

Schemes was already familiar with the entire layout of the bank: its area, its employees, and even where they lived. He'd been scoping the bank since the last takedown. He had watched it open and close. He'd even followed the manager home. After all, his name was Donnie Schemes.

"So what y'all think?" Schemes asked.

Reem leaned forward, between the two seats, and said, "You already know what time it is with me." He was in without even thinking.

They both turned to Ghost, who was rubbing his chin. His eyes were squinted as if he was in deep thought.

"Let me think about it," he told them, feeling the urgency. Reem huffed and puffed and thrashed against the backseat like an angry child.

"Think about it? What is there to think about?"

"Man, I just came home yesterday! What I look like running headfirst in a bank the day after I touched!" Ghost retorted aggressively.

Donnie Schemes butted in.

"I can dig it," he said, nodding. "Just give it some thought. We can get some nice paper outta here."

Ghost nodded his head. He was already considering how much they could come up. He thought about how much his boys came up and what he could do with that kind of bread.

But, in the back of his head, thoughts of Reem's disloyalty were still throbbing. Was he worthy of being trusted? He was ambivalent about committing the robbery with him. He needed to think things over.

Donnie Schemes dropped them back off on Widener Place—a small block of Ogontz Avenue. Widener Street was where it all began. A few years ago, they had set up shop on Locust Avenue, completely muscling the block.

They parted ways. Ghost got in his car, and the other two got in theirs. The Hennessey they had sipped while in Schemes's car hit Ghost as soon as he swung his feet out the car. The Park Avenue rocked back and forth as he recklessly lashed out the parking spot.

He peered in his rearview and saw Reem and Schemes's cars next to one another. Schemes's car was double-parked in the middle of the street next to Reem's. He figured they were discussing the robbery. He knew he had to make up his mind quickly, or they would move without him.

Back at home, he was greeted by Kha at the front door.

"What's up, Ghost?" his little man said with a smile on his face.

Kha was always thrilled to see Ghost. He wasn't his pop, and Kha knew that, but Ghost was there for him as a male figure in his life.

The duties that came along with being that figure were cool with Ghost. He wanted children of his own, but he looked at Kha as his. He was sure Kha looked at him in the same light, but Ghost kept things the way they were supposed to be.

"What's up, little man?" Ghost greeted him back. "What you doing?"

"About to play the game. You wanna play?"

"Yeah, set it up."

At infancy, Kha lost his dad. He was only a few months old when his pop was brutally murdered in the streets. Ghost hadn't known his father personally, but his name had rung a few bells in the city. He was known for getting a little money in the streets.

Some broke, miserable niggas attempted to rob him. They kidnapped and murdered him. Rumors were whispered that he refused to come up off that money, so they killed him. The assailants were apprehended not long after the botched kidnapping.

Even worse, once they were caught, the feds grabbed the case because of the kidnapping, and one of the dudes went in heavy. He made a plea agreement with the government to cooperate for a lighter sentence. He ended up sitting on the other two at trial, and they got the wheel. The rat got a break, getting a180-month sentence.

Ghost knew how tremendous the effect of losing her baby's father was on Kia. A year after the tragedy, they met. She was still grieving with a heavy heart when he came into her life. It took time, but she slowly gave up her excessive mourning.

Ghost played a major part in her healing process. He would hold her in his arms while she wept into the night. This took a lot of strength, care, and love for him to do. He couldn't help the jealous feeling that would arise as she would divert her attention from him to another man. The feeling was senseless, and he would immediately bury it back into wherever it had dug its way out.

Ghost and Kha sat, playing the Play Station 3. He always spent time with him, playing the game, wrestling, or throwing the ball. He'd even taught him how to ride a bike.

Kha had never been subjected to being raised in the hood. Being raised on the outskirts was having a hell of an effect on his upbringing, and he vowed to keep things that way.

"What's your mom doing?"

"She's laying down. She's been sleeping since we got home." Kia maintained a fairly decent job as a sales director for the Hilton Corporation. Between the money she made and the change Ghost pulled in from the streets, they were doing all right.

Once they lost the game, Ghost asked, "Did you do your homework yet?"

"No, not yet."

He grabbed Kha by the top of his head, gave him a gentle rub, and said, "Go get your book bag."

He watched the boy disappear down the hallway to go get his backpack. Suddenly, the thought of the robbery popped back up in his head. The thought wouldn't leave him alone, and he didn't want it to, either.

He thought about that bread again. He thought about Kha and Kia and how they weren't ever victims of poverty. As a man, he felt like it was his job to keep it like that.

He grabbed the phone off the table and dialed a number on the touch screen.

"Yo!" Donnie answered.

"When you tryna move?"

Donnie Schemes laughed at him. "That didn't take long, huh?"

"Man, fuck all the small talk! When you tryna move?" "I'll get with you tomorrow, so we can rap."

"Whatever, man. I need this paper, so let's move ASAP," Ghost said ambitiously.

"All right, all right." Schemes laughed.

The decision was final. Ghost was on a mission. He needed some money. To get it was by any means—even if he had to take it.

CHAPTER 4

The next morning, Ghost was awaken by an eruption of noise as Kia yelled at Kha—something about getting ready for school. It was 6:26 a.m., and Ghost knew he had to meet with his boys this morning, so he got up and got himself together.

The scent of breakfast pervaded the house. Kia was the perfect housewife. She cooked, cleaned, and worked, and the sex was spectacular. The idea of moving in with her couldn't have been a better one. He was feeling like a family man.

Ghost dialed Schemes's number and, when he answered, asked, "What time we getting together today?"

"As soon as possible." Schemes was ready to move.

"All right. I gotta drop my lil man off at school, so let's meet uptown like eight-thirty."

"All right. That's cool."

Ghost agreed to drop Kha off to school in the mornings, and Kia would pick him up in the afternoons. Ghost knew it wouldn't be long before wifey started nagging at him about getting a gig. But Ghost wasn't on that shit wifey was talking about.

35

He liked the layout of the bank and felt good about getting away with the job, so he was banking on that. He entered in the kitchen and found Kia standing at the stove in her robe, whipping up some breakfast.

"What's up, baby?" he said as he grinded up on her ass. "You're pretty excited this morning," she said, feeling him grow hard against her backside. She was naked under the robe, and the grinding aroused both of them.

Kia tilted her head back and hunched her shoulders from the warmth of his breath against her neck.

"Stop, boy," she whined.

Reluctantly, he let go of her and sat at the kitchen table.

After the three of them had breakfast, they left the house. Ghost and Kha escorted Kia to her car like the men in her life were supposed to do.

"Mommy, can Ghost pick me up from school?" Kha asked.

Kia looked at Ghost for his answer. "Not today, little man. I have something I have to take care of, but I promise I will get you sometimes."

Kha nodded his head and showed a little disappointment. Ghost felt bad, but he knew, with the plans today, he couldn't make that promise. If he got booked, that would be one thing, but to let his lil man down would be even worse.

After exchanging hugs and kisses, Kia pulled off in her Chevy Malibu. The simple and modest car was a reflection of her personality.

Inside the Park Avenue, the radio was turned on. Ghost let the radio play on the local morning station. Diggy Simmons eased through the speakers. He cracked up as Lil Kha sang along.

"They be tryna copy and *paaaste* me...I'm on my job."

"What the hell you know about that, little man?" Ghost was getting a kick out of him singing the song.

Kha chuckled. "They be tryna copy and paste me in school." His voice was filled with confidence.

After dropping Kha off, Ghost met up with Schemes and Reem on Widener Place to discuss things before they made their move. They agreed to run down on the bank that morning.

Ghost felt like he was rushing things, but he decided to chase Benjee anyway. When Ghost pulled up, he noticed Schemes and Reem standing by Schemes's car, talking. He could tell they were feeling themselves by the way they were gesturing their hands, putting an emphasis on a conversation that was probably about nothing.

Ghost parked and hopped out. He was draped in all black attire. He was carrying a black, rolled-up ski mask in his hand, and a pair of black cloth gloves overlapped his back pocket.

Reem tapped Schemes and nodded at Ghost. "Look at this nigga," he said with a chuckle. Ghost smirked as he walked up. "What's good?"

"What's up with all the black?" Donnie Schemes asked, pointing at Ghost up and down, wearing a grin on his face.

"What you think is up, nigga?" Ghost retorted with a frown. "Dummy, we robbing a bank! Not doing a cat-burglary." They all laughed at that. Ghost was in all black like they were moving in the middle of the night. It was broad daylight, and the all black could have attracted unwanted attention. At least, it was cold out, and the wind was blowing at a rapid velocity, so he could blend in.

They hopped in the wheel and peeled off. Silence drowned the car as they rode. The radio was off, leaving the sound of the traffic seeping through the cracked windows.

Ghost pondered over Kha and Kia, his freedom, and, of course, that money. The thought of the money still outweighed everything else pulsating in his head. He had to provide, and that was by any means necessary.

The bank got bigger and bigger as it finally came into view. The avenue was paved with cobblestone, and trolley tracks were embedded in the streets. The ride was bumpy, but it was their road to the riches.

The plan was to spin around the bank once to map things out before making a move. They were stuck at the light when they saw the unexpected. The sight wasn't part of the plans. It would definitely affect things.

In front of the bank was a parked armored truck. Two armed guards jumped out the back of the truck with two big-ass bags of money.

Reem rubbed his hands together. "Oh! Look what we have here."

The armored guards scanned the area with a cautious eye as if they could feel danger lurking nearby. Ghost, Schemes, and Reem watched intently as they slid by. One of the guards peered at the car as it went past, and Ghost could have sworn he made eye contact with him. He dismissed his nervousness because there was no way the guard could see through the gloomy-tinted windows.

"Yo! We should jump out on their asses right now," Reem blurted. "I know that truck got something nice in it."

"Yeah, I know," Schemes replied. "But we ain't ready for that right now." Reem sucked his teeth. He was ready to make a move.

"How much you think we can get out of there?" Ghost asked. "Man, did you see those bags? Those joints were husky!" Schemes said excitedly.

The bags were stuffed with paper, but the million-dollar question was, how much? The plan was unfolding even better than they had anticipated.

After parking on a back block for several minutes to allow the armored truck to make its drop and keep moving, they spun the block to scope things one more time.

Things appeared to be just right. Everything was just in place: the truck was gone, commuters were in their own world, and the bank didn't look too crowded.

They parked on the small block at the end of the adjoining driveway. Ghost put his ski mask on his head, but kept it rolled up, so it would look like a skull hat. Schemes and Reem both wore skullies and cut sleeves from a black t-shirt around their necks tucked in their collars.

"Y'all ready?" Schemes asked, releasing a deep breath.

"Ain't no question." Reem was all in.

"Yeah, let's do it." Ghost assured them. He was ready. Butterflies flew through Ghost's stomach as they walked down the dirty driveway. Anxiety flooded his veins as they straddled across the rear parking lot toward the side door of the bank. Ghost searched for any signs of nervousness from the others, but found none.

"Here we go," Schemes mumbled, pulling the sleeve from his collar over his face. Reem followed suit, and Ghost pulled the ski mask down.

They moved in and burst through the doors. The bank's security guard was startled by the masked men. A customer was exiting the bank as they were coming in.

"Get your ass down!" Schemes snagged the dude by his collar and threw him to the ground.

"Get down! Get down!" they shouted in unison.

Fright struck the hearts of the bank occupants. Schemes waved a Mossberg shotgun like a madman. He was a madman. The bank customers and employees dropped to the ground as if he was letting the pump rip.

Ghost leaped over the teller's station while Reem made his way to the vault.

"Where's the manager?" Reem shouted.

Schemes pointed the long weapon at an older white man. "Right there."

The manager looked up, and his head jerked with a bemused look on his face. The thick glasses he wore made his wide eyes look like a fish peering out a fish tank. *How much do they know? How'd they know I was the manager?* he wondered.

Reem read the nametag pinned to his shirt and demanded, "Let's go, Steve!"

Meanwhile, Ghost was behind the counter, collecting the bank scraps.

"No alarms! Take the dye packs and bait bills out! Let's move!" he snapped at the tellers.

The tellers complied without hesitation. Tears trickled down the face of a young black female teller. Her hands trembled as she unlocked the drawers. She quickly removed the dye packs and bait bills. The other tellers followed her procedures.

"Relax. No one is going to get hurt," Ghost assured her, as if that were going to give her some relief.

Relief would come once he took the chrome handgun out of her face. Then, just like that, it was. Ghost jumped back over the counter, giving her the relief she silently prayed for.

Reem was in the vault in awe. Stacks of money were stacked to his midsection. Somehow, he managed to keep moving despite the sight of the money. Carts were filled with the money the truck had just dropped off, but the manager hadn't had a chance to put it up.

Forming his arm in a V-shape, Reem clumsily scooped the money into a large duffel bag. A stack of bills crashed to the floor, scattering all over the vault. Reem greedily started snatching the bills from the floor.

Schemes appeared in the vault's doorway.

"Leave it. Let's go!" he demanded of his man in a shrill tone. "Everyone have a nice day. Thank you for your cooperation," Reem said sarcastically as they fled the bank.

The three of them removed their masks to avoid detection by the outside early-goers. They moved with swiftness across the rear parking lot and vanished down the rubbish driveway.

Doom! Doom! Doom! The doors of the Marauder closed subsequently as they jumped into the bombed out machine. The engine came alive, and the dual exhaust roared with authority. A nebula of smoke and dust billowed from the screeching tires as they peeled out the parking spot, disappearing from the scene richer than they had come.

The take was on!

CHAPTER 5

The grey Expedition swerved through the wooded county roads. The tree-covered trails were deserted as Feeq whipped the truck through the curving lanes. Tia, Feeq's wife, was reclined in the passenger seat and exhausted from a long day at work. Feeq picked her up from work every day. She worked as a home aide out in the county. They, also, resided out in the county shrubs, a nice way from the hood.

Feeq catered to his wife like a real husband was supposed to. He knew he had to buy her some wheels soon because it was tedious picking her up every day after dropping her off in the mornings as well.

But Feeq was as tight as they got. He could squeeze a penny and make it holler, so imagine what he could do to Benjee.

He glanced over at his wifey and asked, "What's up, baby cakes? You're quiet tonight."

"It was a long day. Mrs. Johnson ran me like a race horse today," she complained. "I need a hot shower to relax."

"Daddy will take care of you, baby cakes," he said, rubbing her thighs.

"Ummm...I bet you will." Tia licked her lips seductively. "Have you heard from Reem or Donnie lately?" she asked.

"Naw, I haven't been down that way."

"Good," she mumbled. Feeq just glanced at her for the remark.

By them residing so far away from the hood, Feeq had limited time to be in the ghetto, getting caught up. But trouble followed Feeq wherever he went. It always stayed close by, even in the county where things were covered by trees and land. If Feeq was there, trouble sprouted there as well.

Blue twilight enveloped the sky as the sun crept past its setting. Feeq pushed the pedal to the floor, ignoring the dangers of the curvy roads. Without street lights, the area was a dark forest with roads.

Suddenly, the trees were lit up with red and blue flashing lights. The horn of a police car demanded they pull over.

"Ah, shit!" Feeq snapped.

Feeq pulled the SUV to the shoulder of the road. In what felt like twenty minutes, but was more like two, two uniforms finally got out the car, shining bright flashlights through the tinted windows as they inched closer.

"License, registration, and proof of insurance," the officer said, rapping one hand on the window. He tucked his flashlight and held his pistol.

Feeq mumbled something unintelligible as he leaned over, reached in the glove box, and shuffled through papers. The cop pulled his flashlight back.

"What you say, boy?" the chubby redneck officer said with a dragged accent.

"I have registration and insurance, but I don't have my license."

The officer ripped the door open. "Step outta the car, son." The police violated every constitutional right Feeq had. They searched him, the car, and even violated procedure by frisking his wife, instead of calling a female officer to the scene.

"Yo! Don't touch my wife!" Feeq snapped.

"Shut up, boy!"

The cop rammed Feeq's chest into the truck. Before he knew it, the cuffs were on so tight his hands went numb. He was dragged to the back of the cop car.

Fortunately, they allowed Tia to get back in the truck. After verifying she had a valid driver's license, they decided to let her drive the vehicle home.

They ran Feeq's government through the system. "Looks like you have a bench warrant pending in Philly, son," the cop said as he glared at Feeq.

Feeq tried to talk his way out the back of the car, but the rednecks weren't trying to hear his slick talk. Defeat overcame him, and he sighed, dropping his head to the window.

His mind shut down to all but one thought.

I'm going back to jail.

The latest robbery proceeds tallied a little over $290,000. Ghost, Reem, and Schemes divided the money three ways, leaving each other with nearly a hundred a piece. They hadn't expected to get that much money from the small branch, but, because the hit was right after the armored truck drop, the bank was loaded.

After the take, they hit King of Prussia mall and tightened up their wardrobes. Ghost really needed the upgrade after the skid bid.

Ghost promised to pick Kha up from school. He vowed to himself to never leave him and Kia out on the streets alone to fend for themselves again. A real man stayed on the bricks, taking care of his family, not in jail depending on them.

Ghost knew he was playing with fire by indulging in the bank robbery only a couple days out on the bricks. Even worse, now he was even contemplating flipping the paper in the drug game.

He wanted to take the legitimate route, but the streets were all he knew. Besides, getting into business wasn't as easy as it sounded. A person from the streets with a record had barriers in front of him. Fuck the red tape, more like a red brick wall with graffiti on it saying, "No felons allowed." That was what he believed anyway.

Besides Kha and Kia, Ghost knew he was alone out here. He had so-called homies, but they were just that—so-called. He had lost his mom a few years ago to a heart attack, and his pop was a loser. The only time he'd ever been close to his dad was during a bid where they were in the same facility. He found himself taking care of his pop when things were supposed to be the other way, but he understood his pop had lost the same game he was playing.

Ghost pulled up to the school and saw Kha talking to some little girl. Kha hopped in, smiling ear to ear.

"What's up, little man?"

"Nothing. What's up, Ghost?"

"Why you so happy?"

Kha just smiled and looked out the window. The light-skinned girl he was talking to was still standing there. She waved and blew Kha a kiss. He returned the gesture.

"Damn, little man. I see you got the chicks on you already, huh?" Ghost said, tapping Kha and snapping him out his daze.

Kha just blushed and sunk his small frame into the folds of the seat. Ghost reminisced over his days as a youngin'. He had gone wrong somewhere down the line by getting into the streets. He dreaded that decision and was determined to make sure Kha didn't follow in his footsteps.

"Where we going?" Kha asked, noticing they were headed in a different direction than home.

"Chill. We gon' take a little ride."

Ghost did not want to reveal the secret and ruin the surprise. Ghost and Kia agreed to meet at Jillian's up Franklin Mills. With the arcades, pool tables and bowling alley, they would have a ball. It was family night out.

Schemes and Reem wasted no time investing their money in the game. They had Boyer and Locust rocking. They went half on three bricks. After coming up on two robberies, they both were sitting on well over a hundred a piece.

After fucking up a lot of the money from the first robbery, they decided that they needed to go hard. They had their own block, youngins, and guns, so with the additional money they came up with, they felt untouchable. They asked Ghost if he wanted to chip in, because he was conservative, he said he had to think about it. It was nothing to think about for them—money came first.

"So, how do you want to do this?" Reem asked Schemes, who was standing over a hot stove, watching a pot of water rise to a boil.

"What do you mean?"

"Do you want to give Frog and them some weight or nine-packs?"

"Come on, man! They've been out there with us for a minute, so it's only right we break them off right," Donnie said, a little irritated by the question. "We're going to serve them weight, so they can get all the way on their feet."

The question irritated Schemes because Reem was on some tight shit, and he wasn't feeling that. Frog was Schemes's little cousin, so he wanted to make sure he ate.

"We'll serve Frog and Snook weight, and let them break it down how they wanna do it. We'll break them off equally, and everyone else is separate," Schemes said.

Reem just nodded. He was watching Schemes whip the work in a transparent pot. "Schemes, we should have the old head Pops cook that shit up 'cause it look like you about to fuck that money up."

"Chill! I got it, nigga," Schemes responded, whipping the work like he was pro.

Reem's phone slid across the kitchen table from the vibration of it ringing.

"Yo! Who this?" he answered since he didn't recognize the number.

"You have a pre-paid call ..." the automated machine said "Feeq." Feeq's voice chimed in.

"Oh, shit! Feeq is booked, Schemes," Reem whispered.

His heart was in his ass. The first thought that came to his head was that Feeq somehow got locked up for the first robbery they did. He took the phone away from his ear and looked at it like Feeq could see him.

Reem, hesitating to accept the call, looked at Schemes with an uncertain look.

"Accept the fucking call, dickhead!" Schemes snapped, snatching the phone out of Reem's hand.

He accepted the call. "Yo, unc! What's good?"

"Damn, neph. I've been blowing your jack up like crazy! What's up with you?" Feeq shot, sounding agitated.

"You didn't call my phone."

"Yes, I did. Check your missed calls."

Schemes patted his pockets, but couldn't find his phone.

"Where the fuck is my phone at?" he mumbled to himself.

"What happened? What? You booked?"

Reem stared attentively at Schemes, wanting to know why Feeq was locked up. His nerves started to become jumpy because all he could think about was Feeq being booked for robbery.

"Yo! What he say?" Reem asked in a whisper, a bit jittery. Schemes put up his index finger, indicating for him to hold up. "Holler at Reem for a second. I got some grits on the stove right now," he said in coded language, referring to the coke.

Reem halfheartedly took the phone, fumbling with it before saying,

"Yo, cuz. What's good?"

"Ain't shit. They booked me for a warrant I had on an old drug case yesterday."

"What's your bail?" Reem was relaxed now, knowing Feeq wasn't down for robbery.

"I can't make bail because they dropped a dipsy on me before I could see the warrant unit. They had me in the receiving room all night, but I got Smitty to get me up to the block ASAP."

"Smitty? Who that?"

"You know the CO that mess with my little cousin Taniesha." "Right. I know who you are talking about. You need something?"

"Yeah. I just need you to get with D when he calls, all right?" Reem knew that Feeq was referring to Smitty by his street name. Smitty was his nickname at CFCF because his last name was Smith.

"Yeah, give him my number, and I'll lace you something nice, cousin."

It was understood that Smitty was a horse, and Feeq wanted them to give him a package to smuggle into the prison. It would contain a phone, drugs, and some cigarettes.

Smitty was from the hood, but they didn't deal with him like that because he was a correctional officer. He was a square who tried to act like a gangster.

After making some more arrangements and small talk, they hung up with Feeq. The coke Schemes was whipping was dry and rock hard. They took half of brick out of the one they cooked and broke it down into two nine-ounce batches. Reem called Frog, and told him to meet him at the McDonald's up Stenton Avenue.

After hopping in the Marauder, Schemes found his phone on the side of the driver's seat.

"Damn! Here goes my shit right here," he mumbled, stuffing the phone in his pocket.

"Tighten up," Reem joked.

As they pulled up in the McDonald's parking lot, Reem and Schemes were both startled by the presence of a marked police car parked in front of the adjoining gas station entrance. Frog's car was, also, parked beside one of the gas tanks. Both cars were empty, so they must have been inside the gas station or restaurant.

They kept it moving, driving straight out the parking lot and parking on one of the back blocks. They called Frog and told him to meet them on Beverly Road. There, they would do the pass off.

A few minutes later, Frog parked his Buick Lesabre behind them and jumped in the car with them. Reem handed him the work.

"That's a half of joint in there. It's broke down into two fifties. One for you and one for Snook. They're already fried. Y'all need to learn how to cook, or get Pops to do it for y'all next time 'cause we ain't going to keep doing it for y'all," Schemes said. "All right. I got it. Stop bitching," Frog said in a throaty voice.

He started scratching the back of his throat—his signature.

"Stop that irritating shit with your throat!" Reem snapped. "And like he said, learn how to cook, or you're assed out."

Frog was Schemes's little cousin. The relationship they shared was tight. Schemes only had Frog by two years, so they had been pretty close coming up.

Frog had a raspy voice, and he always scratched the back of his throat, which irritated the shit out of Reem. His voice and scratch sounds resembled those of a frog, so that was where he got his nickname from.

"Y'all need to stop playing and put me on some real paper!" Frog threw his opinion out there to see what their responses would be. It wasn't that he was ungrateful for the work that they had just fronted him, but, in the last week, he'd watched both of them upgrade cars and clothes, and now they were passing off work. He knew they had come up on a sting, but he wasn't sure who or what they had taken down.

"Goak, goak, goak..."

"Man, we'll rap!" Reem said, wanting to get him out the car.

Frog bounced, feeling good. Nine ounces wasn't much, but shit, it was more than he had when he got into the car.

Ghost was sitting on the bed, trying to quickly count the money he wanted to put aside for his plans tomorrow. After the family night at Jillian's, he had stopped down Gratz Street to get some sour diesel. The exotic haze had him and Kia on cloud nine. She was in the shower freshening up.

Ghost was in a hurry to count out $35,000 of the money, so he could hoard it away in a safe tucked under the bed. Copping the exotic smoke had given him an idea. Gratz Street was one of the only blocks that always had the good smoke on a consistent basis. Hustlers from all over the city traveled to Gratz Street to cop off that block because it was so tough to find it anywhere else.

Ghost figured, if he set up a shop uptown, he could take a lot of the clientele from down there and, also, gain his own. He called a Jamaican named Smoke, who always had various loads of weed on deck. Smoke gave him a deal he couldn't refuse: ten pounds of weed for thirty-five thousand. Ghost was hesitant at first to purchase that many pounds because he was starting from the ground, but the offer was too good, and he knew, if things didn't take off right away, he could always get the pounds off wholesale.

Just as he was tucking the safe under the bed, Kia entered, her succulent body cloaked in a towel. Ghost jumped up from the bed suspiciously, drawing the blanket over the stacks of bills on the bed that he'd yet to put in the bag.

Kia squinted her eyes, looking at him suspiciously. Apprehensively, she asked, "What you hiding, boy?"

"Nothing," Ghost said with a guilty smile.

Now Kia wondered about his sneakiness, so she became persistent.

"What you mean 'nothing'? What you pull the covers over?" She snatched the covers off the money before he could

squeeze another lie between his teeth.

"What the—"

Kia threw her hand over her mouth, alarmed at the sight of money scattered on the mattress. "Where the fuck you get all of that money from?"

"Listen, babe. I can explain," he said in a soft voice.

"You fucking right you can explain! You got a lot of explaining to do!"

Tears filled her eyes as she glared at him. Kia didn't care about money. Keeping Ghost with her was all that mattered. She despised the game he was in—the same one that had taken her baby's father.

Ghost started explaining things to her down to the T. Initially, he had planned to hide the money from her and keep her in the dark about his recent endeavors, but now he was compelled to reveal things to her. Either that or lie to her, and that wasn't an option. He always kept it real with her.

Kha was sound asleep in the other room, so Ghost immediately defused the situation, so they wouldn't awaken him. Kia was stuck in an ambivalent state. She had mixed feelings about what he was sharing with her. A part of her was happy he got away, and they had a hundred thousand. But the caring side of her was more concerned about his bad decision, and the risk he took on almost leaving her again. She couldn't believe that he was fresh out of jail and already headfirst back in the game.

"Please, Ghost. Don't do this tomorrow. Please don't leave again," she begged softly.

He took her into his embrace and warmly whispered in her ear that he would never leave them again, trying to soothe her. The relaxing words subdued her. Before they knew it, they were kissing and gyrating against one another. Longing passion overcame them, and they made intense love on top of the big-face money.

Following the sexual episode, Ghost put the money up in a bag and laid there with his queen's head buried in his chest.

Men never listened to their women when they knew they should. His decision was made. The game was calling his name, and, when it called, he had to go.

CHAPTER 6

A month flew by. Time seemed to move at a rapid pace when enjoying life, and life was definitely good for everyone. Ghost's haze-house, which he'd set up on Boyer and Locust Street, at a fiend named Pop's house, was booming. The house was running through over two pounds a day, which brought in roughly twenty grand every day. Dubs of haze moved out the house quicker than Ghost expected. All the hustlers were grabbing on a daily basis, so, after breaking Pops and the youngins he had sitting in the house off, he was pulling in a few grand profit each day.

Schemes and Reem's hustling was reaching new heights as well. They were grabbing five bricks at a time. The strip was moving the work briskly. Frog and Snook were working with half a brick each now. Things looked pretty good for everyone.

Tonight, they were at the strip club, Onyx, down on Delaware Avenue, balling out of control. They almost had to drag Ghost to the club with them. Things with him and Kia were on good terms. She had become more comfortable with his sources of income once he proved how limited his risk of getting caught up was. He spent countless hours with her and Kha, so she was grateful for that.

Meek Mills' *House Party* came blasting through the speakers. The partygoers went crazy as the classic banger played. Two adjoining tables were occupied by their crew. A few dancers surrounded the table, entertaining them.

Bottles of Patrón, Ciroc and Nuvo sat, half-emptied, on the tables. The entire club seemed to be high and tipsy. Smoke permeated throughout the club, creating a fog-like atmosphere. Reem and Schemes were enjoying themselves the most. While Ghost sat back cracking up at them, Reem had an exquisite redbone giving him a lap dance. The redbone worked her hips and ass to the rhythm of the beat like a pro. Reem's face was balled up from the ride she was giving him. He imagined himself inside her the way she was going at it. He could only imagine how her performance would be behind closed doors.

A stripper was on top of the table, working her body like a snake. The caramel table dancer wiggled and popped her ass to every bit of snare and bass in the song. Schemes was making it rain on her ass with stacks of ones. The bitch had a mouth-watering body, and she was working it like she was doing it for TV. When she did her signature move, the club went nuts. She sat on the table and pulled one leg behind her head, holding it with her arms. Flexible was an understatement. While holding her legs in the awkward position, she made her ass clap with a thunderous sound.

"Damn!" the crowd shouted in unison as she performed.
"Oh, shit!" Schemes blurted as he threw the entire stack of
bills at her rigorous ass.

He had to have her after that move. He needed just one shot of her. After her show came to an end, he propositioned her. He wanted to have a quickie in one of the private rooms. Without hesitation, she agreed and took him by the hand. She pulled him toward the secluded rooms. He tapped Reem, giving him a head nod, indicating that he should grab his chick and head to the back with him.

Ghost, Frog, and Snook laughed at them as they watched them slide to the back of the club. They were pissy drunk, throwing ones at some strippers in front of their table.

All the women were putting on that night. They were so caught up in the production that they were unaware of the angry faces across the club, staring in their direction. A thick waitress slid up with a bottle of champagne and approached Ghost.

"This is for you, handsome," she said flirtatiously, licking her lips.

Ghost smiled from ear to ear and, somewhat in shock, asked, "For me, pretty girl?"

"Yeah, from the gentleman over there," she said while pointing across the foggy room.

Ghost squinted his eyes and surveyed the area, looking for the niggas who sent him the bottle. His eyes roamed the room until he found some familiar faces he hadn't seen in a while. He was sure it was them who sent the bottle. *Who else would make an audacious move like this?* Then, he locked eyes with one of them. Ghost smiled deviously, popped the bottle, and raised it to his mouth.

In the private room, Reem had the redbone giving him a private dance. Her hair fell down the side of her face and swung wildly as she popped her body in ways Reem had never seen a woman do before. He drained his stack of ones, paying her for her body-popping performance.

He took her by her hand and said, "Come here, girl."

She obeyed his command by climbing onto his lap. She had to admit to herself that Reem was a cutie. His light skin accentuated his dark black hair. Facial hair sprouted from his round cheeks, taking away from his, otherwise, baby face. Since playing football on Germantown High's team, his body had maintained a nice tone from the countless hours spent in the weight pile. Because of their similar features, people always said he and Ghost looked like brothers.

"How much for some of this pussy?" he asked while rubbing her soaked thong.

"For you, two hundred," she told him like he was getting a bargain price.

Reem knew she had probably been driven up in by Mack truck after Mack truck; however, her gyrating lap dance had blown his mind, so he needed a shot of that.

He peeled five Franklins off his knot and handed them to her. "That's for everything, baby girl."

Without further dialogue, she dropped to her knees and whipped his rock hard dick out. She tore open a condom and used her mouth to put it on. She took his whole eight inches in her mouth, rolling the condom down his entire shaft.

Redbone was a beast.

Reem watched in awe as she sloppily gave him some of the best head he'd ever had. His entire manhood disappeared into her mouth, and she bobbed her head at the bottom like she wanted more to come from his pelvic bone. As she came up to the tip, water flooded her eyes and excess saliva drooled from her mouth, sliding down his shaft. He clawed at the seat as she drove him insane. Her green contacts looked like her real eyes, and Reem was mesmerized by them.

He grabbed her by her hair, twisted her around, and said, "Turn that ass around."

"Oh! You like it rough, daddy," she cooed, using the same words she had used on hundreds of tricks before him.

After ramming his dick in from the back, her ass wobbled up and down. He rushed in and out of her, chasing her as she ran from him. Her light ass turned red as he smacked it. Screams of ecstasy echoed off the four closed in walls.

"Harder, harder, harder!" she cried in excitement.

Reem submitted to her demands, and, for a second, he almost forgot he was pounding a whore. That was how good the pussy was. Mesmerized he thought he was falling in love, but those thoughts evaporated as soon as his scrotum tightened, and he shot his load. Reese and his crew sat across from Ghost and his homies in the hazy club and stared at them. He was amazed at how long they had been watching them without them noticing or feeling the tension in the smoggy atmosphere.

Initially, Reese and his team had been enjoying themselves. Then, Reese spotted the man who had put scars on him months ago. Flashing back, the sounds of the shot rang in his ear, and he could vividly see the grimaced face Ghost wore that day in his head.

Tapping his man C-Note, Reese said, "Look at these niggas." He nodded discreetly in the direction of Ghost and them. In domino effect, C-Note alerted Mil, who in turn made Mar aware of their enemies' presence. The good mood instantly turned sour.

Mar tried to defuse the situation before anything went down. "Fuck them niggas."

"Naw, homie! That nigga has to pay for what he did," Reese retorted with hatred in his eyes.

"What you want to do, homie?" C-Note asked sternly. His tone implied that he was going along with any plan that Reese thought of.

The strippers, who were putting their thing down at the table, felt the attention divert elsewhere. The ones had stopped flying, so the asses stopped shaking. Reese had yet to see Ghost on the streets since he'd been home. People labeled him a rat because of his initial statements to the law about Ghost shooting him. For those reports, Ghost spent six months locked down, but, with the three no-shows to court, Ghost ended up being released.

Word traveled through the streets that Reese was saying he would hold court in the streets. His wish was about to come true. The defendant was sitting there, behind the other end of the opposite table.

Reese tapped the waitress as she strutted by with confidence. "Send those guys over there," he said, making it clear who he was referring to without pointing, "a bottle of Krug Grande Cuvée champagne. Make it clear to them who it was compliments of, would you?" He gave her a thousand dollars in all twenties. The champagne was $900. "Keep the extra as a tip for you." He winked at her and smacked her on the ass when she spun around to walk away.

"That was some boss shit." Mil liked the style of his man. The rest of them nodded in agreement while keeping their eyes focused across the club.

They all sat there and watched the waitress take the bottle to Ghost's table. She seemed to move in slow motion as she served the bottle. They smirked at the puzzled look on Ghost's face as he accepted the bottle.

Ghost's eyes quickly examined the club until his eyes met with Reese's. After their eyes locked, they stared at one another. The long glare seemed to last forever.

The tension was thick enough to cut through with a steak knife as the same thought raced through everyone's head: Now what?

Schemes was in another secluded room, receiving private service from the thick caramel chick. Her body bounced to the Big Sean and Nicki Minaj song that came rumbling through the speakers. She moved rapidly to the fast-paced beat. Her body was flawless. Well, her knees were a little ashy from the dancing, but Schemes didn't care.

He quickly grabbed her and threw her on the couch. He hadn't come back in the private room for a dance. He had seen that shit on the floor. He threw her a few bills which must have satisfied her price tag because she didn't object to him pulling her thongs over her heels.

He pinned her head in her chest and her legs back as far as he could. Surprisingly, she cocked her legs back willingly, locking them behind her head and holding them in place with her elbows. The position was absolutely ridiculous. Schemes was brick hard. Access to her pussy was wide open with her legs so far back. He traveled in and out of her tunnel, reaching her stomach. She whined in pain and pleasure as he fillede her insides with his girth.

The wetness of her pussy made moist sounds as he crushed it. "Oh, my God! Oh, my God!" she cried as he repeatedly hit her spot. "Don't stop! I'm coming!"

Cream filling poured out of her like a fountain, and it covered his manhood. Continuously pumping, Schemes was breathing hard as a runner after a cross-country race. Fascinated by her flexibility, he bent and twisted the whore in all types of positions.

The DJ came over the sound system. "This is DJ Shizzy Mac dripping swagoo on the ones and twos. We're outta here in ten minutes. Thanks for coming out tonight."

At the sound of the warning, Schemes began speeding up his strokes, trying to get what he had paid for. The stripper then took him in her mouth, grabbed his shaft with one hand, and went to work.

She moved her hands rhythmically and slurped simultaneously with spit everywhere. The sordid blowjob drove Schemes crazy. He released in her mouth. Had it not been for the condom, his load would have shot down her throat.

Ghost, Frog, and Snook aggressively worked their way toward Reese's table.

"What's up, nigga?" Ghost snapped.

Ghost had opened and drunk some of the champagne before approaching them. He carelessly flung the half-full bottle on their table and caused a crashing mess.

Reese and his boys lunged from the table, partially to avoid the spilled champagne and fully attempting to get at Ghost. Mar jumped between everyone, stretching his arms out to separate the two groups. "Hold up! Hold up! Hold up!" he shouted. "Not here!"

Besides the music, the club fell silent watching the commotion. Reem was just exiting the back area and saw the commotion. He ran back and got Schemes out of his private dwelling. Schemes came out smiling and buckling his pants, oblivious to what was occurring.

Security came over to break things up and made them take the nonsense outside. The club was about to let out, so they all filed out without a problem.

Outside, it wasn't long before the uproar started again. But now slugs were flying throughout the parking lot. Gunfire erupted, forcing the crowd to breakout in a panic and look for cover.

Reem and Schemes were behind the Marauder, using it for a shield. They were both throwing shots at Reese and his crew, who were behind a Chevy Tahoe, firing back. Reem emptied a chrome handgun while Schemes squeezed off shots from a another.

Frog and Snook had both taken cover. They had learned a lesson: never bring a revolver to a war. They quickly ran out of bullets in their .38 and .44 Bulldog.

Bullets ricocheted off vehicles, making pinging sounds. Glass burst out the Tahoe, raining on Reese and the crew as Ghost emerged from behind the Park Avenue with a TEC .22 with a Swiss cheese nozzle. The TEC released bullets that rapidly left Reese and the rest of his boys balled up behind the truck, taking cover and saying silent prayers.

The Marauder skidded out of the parking spot.

"Let's go!" Schemes shouted from behind the wheel of the bullet-riddled car.

Reem was slouched deeply in the car's passenger seat. Frog dived in the backseat and shut the door.

Ghost hopped in the Park Avenue and screeched out of the parking spot. Snook jumped in the passenger seat, and Ghost passed him the semi-automatic, and he wildly let it rip out the passenger window. Sirens could be heard approaching aggressively.

"Kill them pussies!" Ghost shouted to Snook.

The Park Ave recklessly swerved out the parking lot behind the Marauder. Mil and C-Note jumped from behind the Tahoe, busting at the cars as they escaped the scene.

Boom! Boom! Boom! Click, click, and click. They emptied their guns with rage until the clips were empty.

"Let's get outta here!" Mil shouted.

The innocent partygoers peeped from behind the cars, buildings, or whatever else they had used as shields. They were looking around with terror in their hearts. The parking lot had turned into a warzone. They were happy it was finally over.

All that shooting—nobody hit.

CHAPTER 7

After ripping apart the parking lot the other night, Ghost knew the beef was back on. Reese had played him by sending him the bottle of champagne, and then tried to rock him outside the club. For that, he had to pay.

The streets were buzzing with gossip about the war. Police had said was a drug war on the news. Ghost and his team were dipping and dabbing in the streets. It wasn't that they were scared. Instead, they were cautious because the men they were at war with were just as ruthless as them. They showed heart by busting their guns, so now they all knew it was on sight, and the first ones caught slipping could pay with their lives.

Ghost had an advantage, though; he had more money than Reese and his squad put together. This gave him the edge on them. He could easily supply his weed spot from a distance while they probably had to come around to chase a dollar.

Reem and Schemes could do the same. They laid in the cut, but continued to flood the block with work. Frog and Snook, on the other hand, were more open for an attack because of their close dealings with the block. Laying low wasn't an option for them. They felt like the rest of them were being pussies and copping out with the excuse of playing things safe. What Frog and Snook failed to understand was that, in war, strategy was critical.

From the way things were unfolding, it appeared Reese and his boys were playing things a little safe as well. None of them had been spotted for the last few days. It was more likely they would show face first because they had to come to the hood to eat. Dozens of people were on standby and were told to notify Ghost and them if any of them were spotted. For now, the guns were loaded, and they could do nothing but wait, so they did.

Schemes had to purchase some new wheels because the Marauder had gotten tore out the frame at the club shootout. Bullet holes had penetrated the car all over. Schemes thought about how, if the car wasn't there for a shield, he would have gotten downed.

"How much for the Range Rover over there?" Schemes asked the salesman at the B&D Motors on Broad Street.

"Forty-nine thousand dollars," the salesman responded wryly, like the price tag was too much for Schemes to handle.

"I'll take that and the black Buick Century over there."

"Sir, we'll have to do an extensive credit check for approval for both cars. We'll need proof of income and all. Are you prepared to do that today?" the salesman asked with a hint of doubt in his tone.

Schemes was dressed in a navy blue Dickies set and black Timberland hiking boots. Normally, he wouldn't wear either, but the war was on, so he strayed away from the pretty boy fashion. The dirt parking lot had his boots covered with dust, so he looked like a crumb from the bottom of the earth. Because of Schemes's appearance, the salesman had made the wrong idea about his status and was being quite rude.

Schemes knew about the crooked, under-the-table dealings the auto dealer was used to doing, so he came fully prepared to complete such a transaction. The contents in the bag were more than enough to persuade the dealer to modify the paperwork into saying a large lump sum wasn't put down to avoid attention from the feds.

"Let's go inside and talk," Schemes told him.

Inside, Schemes unzipped the bag and put a few stacks of money on the man's desk. For a second, his eyes were glued to the money.

"Put that away," he said with a quick, dismissive wave of his hand. He looked around sneakily at the other employees and customers to make sure no one had peeped that. Then, he looked back at Schemes and said, "Let's get down to business."

He rubbed his hands together as a smile spread across his face. All he could think about was his commission.

Schemes negotiated the purchase of both vehicles for forty thousand in straight cash. He broke the happy salesman off with a nice tip for his dirty work. They agreed that he could come back to get the Range, but, for now, Schemes hopped in the bombed-out squatter he'd brought solely for going to war in.

"Somebody got to die!" Biggie Smalls played from the speaker as soon as he popped the disc in and pulled off.

Later that night, Reem, Schemes, and Ghost were all home, chilling, when Reem got a call from some chick named Toya from down the way. She told Reem that C-Note was out and about like nothing was going down. Even worse, he was only a block away from where they got money at. C-Note was in TJ's Lounge with some woman nobody supposedly knew, according to Toya.

Reem, Ghost, and Schemes quickly met up to put together a plan to put C-Note down. Frog and Snook weren't answering their phones. That was kind of strange, but it wasn't the time for worrying about why they kept getting their answering machines. It was time to put some work in.

Dressed in dark clothing, they all rolled together in Schemes's blacked-out Buick Century. With dark tinted windows and no hubcaps, the car looked like a death-mobile. The music was cut off, leaving utter silence in the car.

Clanking sounds echoed as they strapped up with heavy artillery. The same TEC .22 was loaded with bullets to the tip. Reem sat in the back with a Mossberg 500 shotgun loaded with eight large rounds. Schemes kept it simple with a Glock .17 handgun, but he was well-prepared with an extended thirty-three shot ladder.

They were heated, the way they were laying low, playing things safe. This nigga C-Note had the audacity to be in the bar, flaunting with some chick on his arm. He was just as wild as Frog and Snook were, so he didn't give a fuck about laying low.

They pulled their hoodies over their heads as they were bending the corner at Boyer and Locust. They were about to turn up Boyer Street toward Woodlawn when Reem's phone started ringing. The screen displayed Toya's name.

"This is Toya again," he told them.

"Man, we're here now. Call her back after this," Schemes said, turning the corner.

They were startled when they saw what awaited around the corner. Their hearts dropped to their asses.

Red and blue lights glimmered off TJ's Lounge and the brownstones. A crowd of nosy observers hovered behind yellow and black caution tape and shouting police. Black and yellow cones were scattered throughout the scene, marking shell casings. Two white sheets were pulled over two lumps of dead weight. The lifeless bodies sent a chill up Ghost's spine.

The three of them looked at one another with confusion, and Ghost knew they were feeling and thinking the same thing he was. Frog and Snook weren't answering their phones.

Was it them two under the white sheets?

C-Note was in the bar, feeling himself. The .40 Caliber tucked under his shirt emboldened him even more. He was accompanied by a bad Rican chick, so he was being flashy tonight. He brought bottles for several people he knew in the bar just to show off.

C-Note had gotten his nickname because his craftiness at duplicating money. Counterfeit money was his hustle. He was known for circulating his fake money, but, in the hood, he never burnt nobody with the suspect bills. He'd pop them off elsewhere, and show off in the hood with money. He was a flashy guy. Tattoos covered his arms, back, and neck, emphasizing his crazy demeanor.

C-Note knew the beef was on, but he felt like no one was going to run him out of his hood. Shit, the way things were looking, Ghost and them were too scared to show their faces. With any movement they did, the .40 Cal would blow. That was his word.

"What's up, baby? You ready to skate?" he asked the 'Rican mami.

"Whatever you want to do, papi," she slurred.

C-Note gave his goodbyes to everyone as he worked his way to the exit. His dime piece followed closely behind, switching her ass and turning her head. He had never paid Toya, who was in the back of the bar on the phone, any attention.

The liquor hit them as soon as they came to their feet, evidenced by the broken swagger in their walks. The late night breeze smacked C-Note right in the face as soon as he got outside.

He hit the alarm on his keychain, unlocking the doors to his pearl white Escalade. Two figures appeared in his peripheral vision. He looked to see Frog and Snook, crossing the street, heading toward the bar. He flinched like he was about to grab the burner off his waist and let it rip on them, but he had to think twice because mami was with him. He couldn't body two people while she was right there.

Frog caught the sudden move out the side of his eye and turned to see C-Note crossing the street. His heart dropped from the surprise sighting one of the men who had tried to kill him days earlier.

Frog pulled his gun out, and Snook followed once he saw C-Note. C-Note tried to shove the chick out the way and pull his forty out, but the hesitation was all it took for him to lose his life.

Gunshots rang out, and bullets traveled at the speed of light. C-Note's frame was riddled with shots instantly. His body jerked and crashed to the ground. Mami's screams were louder than the gunshots. Her eyes widened like she'd just taken a hit of a glass dick.

She stared into the gunmen's eyes, looking for some compassion, but the bearded men raised their guns to her after downing the lifeless drunk.

"Please don't kill me!" she begged, shaking her head back and forth. "I have kids!" she pleaded.

But her cries went on deaf ears. It was too late. She was in the wrong place at the wrong time. They had to let her have it because she'd seen their faces.

They looked at each other and shrugged their shoulders. Mami's body started hemorrhaging from the slugs pumped in her stomach and chest cavity. She coughed up blood and gagged as it spouted out her mouth.

After Frog and Snook stepped over their bodies and put a few more in her sputtering face and C-Note's dead body, they fled through a dark debris-infested alley.

C-Note went out like a gangster, with a pocketful of money, a pretty woman by his side, and his burner in his hand.

But hesitation had cost him his life. He never even got a shot off.

CHAPTER 8

After the murders of C-Note and his Puerto Rican beauty, homicide detectives and marked patrol cars started crawling through the hood. Pressure was being applied to all the hustlers and anyone else who may have had some info about the gruesome double murder.

Toya was one of the ones questioned since she was in the bar moments before C-Note and his dime piece walked out to their fates. Toya stood tall, though, not mentioning a word to the law. Homicide detectives couldn't care less about the murder of the convicted felon, but, since someone murdered a mother of two, they combed the hood for clues.

Since the incident two days ago, Reem and Toya had started kicking it more. She'd been feeling him, but he just started giving her play after her assistance to him and lack of assistance with the law. Initially, Reem was only playing her close to make sure she didn't cooperate with the cops, but, after she performed some wild things behind closed doors, he was wide open.

"You going to drop me off at work tonight, baby?" she asked Reem.

"Yeah, what time you gotta be there?"

"Eleven o'clock." Toya was a manager at Walmart. She had been a manager there for the last year and a half.

She'd spent the last two nights with Reem. They had stayed at one of his apartments in the Northeast because he wasn't ready to show her where he laid his head.

He watched as she swung her petite, perky ass out the bed and wobbled out the room. He flew out the bed and followed her into the bathroom. She stood in the bathroom mirror, combing her hair as he grabbed her from behind. He planted his face in her neck, kissing her soft spot.

Squirming from the sensation, she said, "You better stop, boy. You know I can go all day." He'd just finished dusting her off in bed.

"So can I." He twisted her around and threw her up on the sink.

Slowly entering her with the tip of his dick, he gave her little strokes until her wetness increased. She clenched him tightly with her hands around his neck and legs around his waist.

Her muffin swallowed him whole as he thrust in and out of her. She tilted her head back, leaning it against the sink-top mirror. Reem started dominating her with long, hard strokes. Glaring at his reflection in the mirror, he balled his face up fiercely as he tried to crush the pussy.

Toya was past moaning from ecstasy—she was now crying from the pleasurable pain.

"Beat this pussy up! Beat this pussy up!" she begged.

"Whose pussy is this?" Reem asked, wanting his name tagged on the new piece.

"It's yours, baby! It's yours, Reem!" she assured him. "I'm cumming! Don't stop! Don't stop! Please!"

Her whimpering and sexual pleas aroused Reem even more. He gave her all he had in the tank. He was trying to lock this pussy in—it was so good. She clenched her legs around him even tighter as if he was going somewhere. Her cream filling gushed out, soaking and dripping down his balls.

Continuously pumping, Reem was nearing an explosion. She drowned him as he swam in her internal pool. He pulled out of her and snatched her by her hair, yanking her off the sink and sitting her on the toilet.

By her hair, he held her head back with one hand. With the other, he stroked himself. Toya looked up at him, loving his aggressiveness. He stared in her eyes and was mesmerized by her exotic hazel pupils. Reem had a thing for chicks with pretty eyes, and Toya's eyes were accentuated by her caramel skin.

She caught every drop of his nut as he busted all over her face and mouth. She stuck her pierced tongue out and let the nut drip all over her lips and slide down her chin. The nastiness drove Reem crazy. He was falling in love with her already. Things were too good to be true.

With her fingers, she slurped his cum up and swallowed it. While looking in his eyes and sending him into a deep trance, she smacked her mouth and opened it to show him that she didn't leave a drip.

Later that night, Toya climbed out the car and sauntered into the department store, heading to work.

"I love that bitch," Reem mumbled to himself as he watched her look good in even the Walmart uniform. "I definitely gotta upgrade her," he said, continuing the one-way conversation with himself.

Toya wasn't even driving at the moment. Her car was broken down. The piece-of-shit had been parked in front of her house for a minute. Reem decided he had to upgrade not only her, but his bullshit Crown Vic, as well.

Caught in a daydream, he was snapped back to reality by his ringing phone.

"Yo!" he answered.

"Where you at?" Frog asked frantically.

"Not far. What's good?" Reem asked nervously, picking up on the tone of his man.

"It's Snook, man," he said, sniffling.

"What the fuck happened to Snook?" Frog continued to sniffle, and Reem repeated himself. "What the fuck happened to Snook?"

Mar, Mil, and Reese emerged from hiding after the murder of their boy. The art of war was to be deceptive, but they said, "Fuck deception right now." Their boy was dead, so somebody had to pay. They were going straight at Ghost and his crew.

They rode in a navy blue Pontiac Grand Prix with tinted windows. The music was down low but loud enough to hear. Meek Mill's *Tupac Back* eased through the speakers—just right for the mood to catch a body.

Huh, Tupac back, I'm two Glocks strapped.

Rolling down in Philly this the new Iraq.

Meek spit words that couldn't be more to the point. Bodies fell everywhere in the violent city. Each year, murders bypassed the number of days in it. Tonight, death was in the air, and, if left up to them, the total would most certainly rise.

Darkness invaded the sky as they cut through the traffic silently. They hoped to catch them out on Boyer and Locust Street. It didn't matter who was out there. They were getting hit tonight.

The headlights lit up the block as the Grand Prix slowly crept down it. The block was dead—nobody appeared to be out.

They didn't notice Frog and Snook sitting in the parked Buick LaSabre, serving their youngins some work. Frog and Snook didn't see them either as they drove by.

While they were at the stop sign, they saw someone coming down the steps of the weed house. It came to Reese like an epiphany when he saw the customer coming out the spot.

"Yo! We're running up in the drug house," he said firmly.

"Let's go," Mar responded. They parked the car down the block and walked to the weed house like regular customers. Stiz, playing the doorman, opened it as if everything was normal. The nozzle of the Mac startled him as it was stuck in his grill.

"Don't fucking move!" Reese told him, pushing him through the doorway. Reese took the burner off Stiz's waist, and Mar and Mil barged through the door, making demands for the men and woman tricking to get down.

"Where's the shit?" Reese shouted.

"Under the couch," one of the chicks screamed after none of the dudes answered.

I'm Reese and his crew weren't stick-up boys, so their robbery game was sloppy. They didn't even have a bag to put the shit in. They didn't even have masks, gloves, or anything else to hide their identities. They were slipping so much that they didn't even check the house to see if anyone else was there.

They used wires from the remote controls and plugs from the video game to tie everyone up. They dumped out a couple of sneaker bags and stuffed the bread and work in them.

"Tell Ghost I did this to him," Reese said arrogantly to one of the gagged men on the floor. Dude mumbled something smart in return.

"What, pussy?" Reese snapped and smacked him ferociously with the four-pound.

"Chill, nigga. We're outta here," Mil said, grabbing Reese off dude.

Just as they were about to leave, they heard a sound in the kitchen that sounded like plates clanking together. They started to ignore it and roll, but all hell broke loose when a dude barged from the kitchen, chopping on them. Reese and Mil got hit and dropped instantly.

Mar hit the gunman up before he could hit him, too. Blood painted the walls like a gruesome horror movie, leaving splatters everywhere. Mar, then, struggled to pull Mil off the floor, but it was a done deal for him.

Reese jumped up, staggering, and helped Mar with Mil, but he saw it was too late—fate had called his name. His eyes stared blankly at the ceiling.

"Let's go, man. It's over. He's gone," Reese said emotionally. Mar didn't want to accept that his homie was gone—another one.

"He's gone! We have to get outta here!" Reese said more aggressively.

Mar reluctantly gave in. There was no time for weeping right now. Mar started to kill all the hostages, but thought against it. The war was far from over. In fact, it was just the beginning. As soon as they got outside the house, more shots rang out.

Snook and Frog were parked under a tree, escaping the dim lights. They were serving two of their customers some bundles when they heard the shots going off close by. The shots were muffled, but they were sure it was somebody letting off. Panicking, they grabbed their weapons.

"Are y'all strapped?" Frog asked Ronnie and Kyle, two of their young hustlers, who were in the backseat.

"Naw, we ain't bring no burners out the crib," Kyle said.

Frog shook his head. "All right. Get the fuck outta here," he told them. "It sounds like that came from the weed spot," he told Snook.

They all jumped out the car. Ronnie and Kyle ran off 'round the corner while Frog and Snook crept toward the weed spot. As they got closer, they saw two figures running down the steps with bags and guns in their hands.

From the rip, they knew they must have just robbed the spot. Without hesitation, they started shooting at them. The robbers were caught off guard, but were lucky enough not to get hit. They dipped behind the parked cars and started shooting back at them across the street.

Frog swore to himself that one of the dudes looked like Reese. *It has to be him*, he thought, but he couldn't make out his face because he had to keep taking cover as the bullets whizzed by.

The two robbers were obviously trying to retreat because they kept inching further down the block as they periodically let off a few shots. Snook made a brave move as he jumped out from behind the parked car and walked in the street, trying to hit them while they were getting in their car.

"Ha!" Snook hollered, going mad trying to down something. Frog was out of bullets, so he couldn't do anything but lie back in the cut and pray. Snook hit one of the dudes as he was getting in the car. Though the dude stumbled in the door well, the bullets seemed to be bouncing off his chest like he had a vest on. Snook ran out of bullets and was stuck with nowhere to go once the other dude started chopping back.

"Snook!" Frog screamed with a raspy tone. Everything moved in slow motion as he watched his man get riddled with bullets. The air seemed to stop flowing as he watched it taken out his man's body. He was sure it was Reese who'd just killed Snook. He'd gotten a good look at his face as life slowed down.

Snook's body jerked and twisted like he was doing the Harlem Shake and crumbled to the ground.

Sirens could be heard but seemed like they were on the other side of the earth. Frog couldn't believe his eyes. Tires screeched, and Frog knew the shootout was over.

But this was war.

CHAPTER 9

The murders of Snook, Mil, and the dude in the weed-house had the block on fire. Ghost and his boys wanted to avoid getting burnt by all costs. Police swarmed Boyer and Locust, investigating for weeks. This approach by the police shut down the progress of the block. Fiends disappeared, and the haze spot was sealed off by yellow and black tape, virtually shutting the moneymaker down.

Snook's funeral was dark. They still couldn't believe he was gone. Kia sensed things weren't right with Ghost. He had seemed so distant from her and Kha for the last few weeks. It was like he was there physically, but, mentally, he was someplace else. She wondered where. Initially, she thought it was because of Snook getting killed, but now she was starting to think it was more than just that.

Today was another one of those angry mornings. Ghost seemed to have awaken on the wrong side of the bed. The previous night had been no different. He had gone to sleep on the wrong side, too. Their sex life had taken a hit.

Kia draped her robe around her body and came swaying out of the bathroom and into the bedroom. Ghost was sitting on the edge of the bed, staring at the TV. It was more like he was staring straight through the screen and not recollecting anything on it. Kia took her robe off and revealed her sexy body; Ghost, seemingly, wasn't the least bit interested; he didn't even glance at her. His lack of attention was killing Kia, and she was sick of it.

"What's your problem?" she asked with a hint of frustration in her tone.

"Nothing. Why? What's up?" he answered without taking his eyes off the TV.

"What's up? What's up? You're what's up, nigga!" The explosion was built-up personal and sexual frustration.

Kia believed he was cheating on her, but little did she know that she was misreading the entire situation. Confusion boggled her head.

She poked Ghost in the temple with her index finger, emphasizing her words. Ghost grabbed her by her hand and flung her to the bed. Using his body as leverage, he fell on top of her to avoid being pummeled by her rage of swinging. Kia punched, kicked, and scratched at her distant lover. Anything to make him feel the pain she was feeling.

"What the fuck is your problem?" he asked, while she was still pinned to the bed.

Kia started crying and screaming at the top of her lungs, "Who is she? Who is she?"

Kia could have sworn Ghost was fucking someone else. Watching too much *Maury* was getting to her or something because Ghost wasn't even cheating on her. But the things that were taking place in the streets were drilled in his head, disrupting his personal life.

"Who is who? What are you talking about?" Ghost asked, confused by her absurdity.

He still held her tight because, even though she had stopped trying to attack him, he wasn't sure if her rampage was over.

"The bitch you're fucking!" she retorted, staring holes into him.

"What? Is that what this is about? Are you serious?" he said, easing his hold but matching her leering.

"Don't play dumb with me!" Kia snapped again. "You're fucking someone else 'cause you're not fucking me!"

Finally, he let her go and sat on the edge of the bed, burying his head in his hands. Using his fingers, he massaged his temples and let out a long sigh, trying to get rid of the overwhelming tension.

"Listen, babe, I know I've been acting funny lately." He faced her. "But one thing you never have to worry about is me fucking with some other bitch."

Kha appeared in the doorway. The noise had disturbed him, and, like a superhero, he'd rushed in to rescue his mom.

"Why are you crying, Mommy?" he asked with his fists balled up by his sides.

"I'm fine, baby. Finish getting ready for school," she squeezed out between sniffles.

Kha shot Ghost a devious look through squinted eyes. Reluctantly, he vanished down the hallway.

"Listen, babe," Ghost said as he took Kia's hands. "I'm just going through a lot right now, but believe me—nothing is more important to me than you and Kha," he said, wiping away the tears traveling down her cheeks.

Ghost felt like a piece-of-shit because his life in the streets was tearing his home life apart. Kia added to the battering. Her stubbornness wouldn't even allow him to give an explanation. She wasn't trying to hear anything.

"Then, act like it!" she retorted and stormed out the room.

Reese and Mar were feeling the loss of their homie, Mil. Although they killed two men from the other side, they still felt like they hadn't done enough. First, seeing C-Note and then Mil in a casket was an unbearable feeling. Even worse was seeing Mil, lying in a pool of blood and with his lifeless eyes still open, haunted them. It reminded them of death and how close the reaper was.

The way things had happened was like something they'd seen in movies, forcing them to live it. It was nothing like the big screen, though, because bullets flew and people died.

Reese thought about how his life was spared by the Kevlar bulletproof vest he was strapped in that night. Between the weed house and outside, he had gotten hit a couple of times. Luckily, he escaped the episode with only a chest full of black and blue bruises. He'd already experienced the pain of hot slugs piercing his body when Ghost hit him. His wounds reminded him of that burning sensation and thoughts of it made him furious every time he thought about it.

"Yo! Word is Reem's fucking the bitch Toya from up the way now," Mar told Reese.

"Yeah?" Reese was surprised by and interested in the news. "Wasn't that bitch there the night C-Note got hit?" he asked skeptically.

"Yeah, as a matter of fact, she was," Mar said, squinting his eyes and tilting his head. "I remember they said she was one of the ones the law grabbed for questioning."

"Then, all of a sudden the nigga start fucking her, huh?" It was more of a statement than a question by Reese.

"Something don't sound right about that shit."

Mar rubbed his chin and contemplated. "You think she had something to do with that shit?"

"I don't know. When was the last time you seen that bitch?"

"I haven't seen her in a minute, but word is she still works at Walmart at Cedar Brook Plaza."

They locked eyes and sat in silence for several long seconds. They were thinking the same thing.

Reese put it in words anyway. "Let's grab that bitch since we can't find them bitch-ass niggas."

Mar just nodded his head.

Reem and Toya had gotten a bit more serious over the last few weeks. After the bodies dropped in domino effect, Reem had to keep a low profile, so he stayed away from the hood to duck the law and to be sure not to get caught slipping. Reese and his crew were obviously going hard and moving on them with no rap, so he was trying to watch his body.

Toya was happy that Reem was laying low because he was spending a lot of time with her. On the outside looking in, she knew Reem was getting a couple of dollars, but, once she was with him, she got to see firsthand that he was heavy.

"I'm getting you a car tomorrow," Reem told her.

"Oh, yeah? What kind, baby?"

"I don't know. Something nice, though. Anything, so I don't have to keep dropping you off and picking your ass up all the time."

She laughed at that. "Whatever, nigga."

"You need to quit that nothing-ass gig anyway." "Not now, baby. We'll talk about this later."

Reem had been trying to convince her to quit the job at Walmart. He wasn't feeling her still working there because he felt like he could take care of her, or she could get something better. She'd been there for four long years and had been a manager for a year and a half, so she wasn't ready to quit just like that. It was only a shaggy department store gig, but she was cool with her co-workers, and her shift was at night, so it was sweet. Reem wasn't trying to hear none of that shit; he wanted her to quit.

"All right. I love you, baby," she said, climbing out the car.

"Love you, too, baby," he told her after a long kiss.

He was dropping her off at the back door of the department store where the third shift entered to go to work since the store was closed. After Toya went inside, Reem got out the car to take a leak.

While draining himself behind the dumpster, he was startled by a sudden crashing sound and a shadow moving in a dimly lit area. He froze in place, forcing himself to bring his urine to a stop. He leaned back to see a Walmart employee swinging trash bags over his head into the dumpster. He watched the man go back inside and carelessly shut the door without watching his surroundings. Reem wouldn't have thought nothing, but the employee didn't even know he was behind the dumpster. His robber instincts kicked right in, and he knew the take would be sweet.

As he drove home, he recalled that the Walmart up northeast had been taken down a few years ago. Robbers donning Walmart uniforms had robbed it late at night. According to the news and word on the streets, they got away with around $350,000.

Come to find out, it was an inside job, and the manager who lined the robbery up broke, and they all got booked after he told. Reem thought about how sweet it would be to take the department store down. He already had an inside person—Toya.

First, he had to find out a few things from her: how many people were there at night and where the money was located. He knew he and his team could wait patiently outside in the trenches of the darkness until one of the employees brought the trash out. They could slide right up on him and gain entry in seconds. With the holidays rolling around, the store had to be loaded, and they could clean house.

Reem smiled to himself as it all came together in his head. It was perfect, and he couldn't wait to call his boys. He dialed Ghost's number, but, after getting no answer, he called Schemes. Donnie Schemes wasn't the only one who could put shit together.

CHAPTER 10

Ghost, Reem, and Schemes agreed to take down the Walmart store, but the job wasn't as simple as it seemed. They needed to do some homework on the store first, so they wouldn't go in blind. Taking money was in their blood, so, naturally, they were with the take, but they wanted things put together thoroughly before they moved.

Toya was the easiest way to find out the things they needed to know. Reem felt like they could be straight up and ask Toya about the store and tell her about the plan, but the others weren't with it. Over Reem's objections, Ghost and Schemes made him agree to pick her head indirectly.

"We can't trust that bitch." Schemes had emphasized. However, Reem felt differently. He didn't think it was because of his feelings for her, but, because she stood up about C-Note being murdered, he felt like she could be trusted. But the others weren't feeling his position, so he had to find another way to get it out of her.

First, they needed to know where the safe was at. That bread was the main priority. How many people worked the third shift was what they needed to know next. Because Reem was bitching about taking it down while she was there, they needed to find out when she would be off, so they could commit the robbery that night.

"Man, we can tie that bitch up, too!" Schemes said.

Reem wasn't feeling tying his little chick up. Fuck the other employees, but he wasn't doing his chick dirty.

Because of the holiday shopping season, the store was bound to be loaded with paper. Now, they just had to put everything together and execute. Reem was lying in bed with Toya cupped in his arms. She'd just finished one of her mind-blowing performances. Reem knew right then was the perfect time to start picking her head. What better time to do it than after some hot sex? She was open and gullible.

"Baby, have you been thinking about quitting your job like I've been asking you to?" he asked while sounding genuine about wanting her to quit.

"Come on, baby. Do we have to go through this again?" Reem knew she didn't want to keep touching this topic, but

he knew he could get her talking, so he pressed. "I'm just saying, babe. It's no need for you to work there no more."

"I told you. It's not all about the money. I've been there forever, and I got friends there."

"Friends? What friends? How come I haven't met them yet?" he asked sarcastically.

"My girlfriend Rita and my buddy Ryan work there." "Ryan?" His antennas went right up at the mention of a dude. "Trust me. Ryan is no one to be worried about," she said with a giggle like the it was funny.

That got Reem's blood boiling.

"What the fuck is so funny?" he snapped. "Who the fuck is he then?" he asked.

Things started to heat up when he became aggressive. He was putting on one hell of a show, pretending to be overly concerned about her quitting. After hearing about the dude Ryan, he pretended to become furious.

Toya immediately went for the rouse and got hyped.

"Ryan is just another manager there. He works in the manager's office. He counts the money and handles all the checks and shit like that," she said dismissively.

"So, what? You want to stay there because of him then?" He frowned as he asked the question.

Toya's buttons were being pressed now. Since she'd been with Reem, she hadn't even considered cheating on him with another man. Even if she did, Ryan would be the last person he had to worry about. It bothered her that he was questioning her loyalty.

"No, I barely see him! I only see him in the break room!"
"Oh, so you be having lunch with him, huh?" Reem was losing focus of his goal and the purpose of the argument.

"As a matter of fact, we do!" she said with a hint of sarcasm. "Me, him, Keisha, Rita, and the five other people on the shift!"

Oh, this was perfect, even easier than he expected. Her last revelation about how many people worked on her shift brought Reem back to reality.

Toya was a blabbermouth when she got angry. She was known for holding water, but get her mad and throw in a little trickery, and she would start running off at the mouth like any other female.

Reem played along, continuing to appear upset. He still needed a little more to come running out her motor-mouth, and he was sure it would.

"Come to think about it..." He squinted his eyes as if he was trying to recall something. "You were a little happy the other day when I took you to get your check! What? Was that Ryan in the office you went in?"

"No! Ryan works my shift, dick-head!" Toya's mouth was crazy. Reem took the verbal abuse on the chin. "The day shift manager was there giving out checks," she added.

Little did Toya know she had just given him all the info he was looking for. "All right! Whatever! Leave it alone! Go ahead and be some busted-ass Walmart worker!" Reem was trying to end the fight because he'd gotten what he was looking for, but he couldn't end it without sliding in an insult of his own.

Toya finally let it go after a little more ramming. She laid in the bed and tried to distance herself from him and make an imaginary line between them.

Reem laid with an invisible smirk. He knew that about nine people worked the third shift, where the manager's office was, and who the manager was. Now, all he had to do was find out when Toya would be off. He'd find that out tomorrow once she was cooled off. For some reason, he couldn't stop thinking about who Ryan was. *Why is she holding onto this job? Is she fucking this nigga?*

Schemes and Frog were playing each other close lately. Since Reem mentioned the idea of robbing Walmart, a few days flew by. Schemes loved the idea of the job, especially since he wasn't really hustling the way he was when the block was jumping.

He felt like it was true that someone couldn't get money and go to war at the same time. Then again, it depended on how he was getting money. He was from uptown, and anyone who knew dudes from uptown knew somehow they had a reputation for taking money and being pretty boys. Hustling was just his side thing to pull in a few extra dollars until the next take.

Now, Schemes was feeling all the shit Ghost had been talking about, about how they needed to invest their money in something legit. Ghost preached that shit, but it wasn't like he had a 401K plan or some hefty portfolio. But now he was digging what Ghost was saying about being prepared for the future and always being ready for the storm when it's sunny outside.

The Range lurched through traffic like a madman was behind the wheel. Well, there was a madman behind the wheel. Another one was buried in the heated passenger seat. Frog was reclined, smoking a Dutch.

Frog was always on go time, but, lately, he had started to listen about being smart and playing things safe. After losing Snook, he realized how vulnerable he was. Being tough did not mean he had to be on the frontline to let the hood know he wasn't scared. People knew none of them was shook by their reputation and the way bodies dropped like flies. Fuck the streets. They were always going to whisper, so let them. Ghost, Reem, and Schemes had, finally, got this drilled into his head.

"Yo! What's up with taking something down?" Frog asked, breaking the silence of the two by turning the radio down to ask Schemes.

"I don't know, Frog. I'm trying to tread lightly," Schemes lied. "Man, you've been brushing me off on that shit forever," Frog retorted a bit offensively. "You'll move with Ghost and them, but not me. I'm supposed to be your family!"

Lately, Frog had been bugging Schemes about taking some money. He wanted desperately to take something after his paper slowed down. He wasn't sitting on paper like the rest of them were, so he had to do something to get at a dollar. If they didn't put him in sooner or later, he had some ill thoughts at going at one of them. Shit! When personal interest was at stake, it was every man for himself. If a man in the game didn't know that, he was bound to be ruined.

Schemes was skeptical about losing his standards by moving with Frog. Though he was his little cousin, he wasn't the type of person he wanted to do certain things with. He was too reckless and careless.

Schemes felt bad for dragging him along. He had been spoon-feeding Frog for a minute now, and he knew that he should put him on some real money. His guilt had made him consider doing a job with him, but not the Walmart one.

"I'll see what I can put together for us," he told Frog somewhat forcefully.

Feeq laid back in his cell and stared at the dull white walls. Graffiti of various tags adorned the wall and repped different sets. Time was flying by, and it wasn't looking like the gates would be cracking anytime soon. He had paid his lawyer a healthy piece of change, but, so far, the high priced mouthpiece had only uttered broken promises. Motions for his probation violation detainers to be lifted had been denied twice. This made him somewhat complacent with the inevitable—that he'd be down for a minute.

A light tap on his cell door caught his attention. CO Smitty opened the door without waiting for Feeq's acknowledgement.

"What's good with you?" he asked, closing the door behind him.

"Ain't shit, man. Little stressed out. That's all," Feeq responded, a bit depressed from the circumstances.

"I can dig it, homie. You gotta chill when you get back out there this time," he told Feeq seriously.

Smitty was a correctional officer, but he was still from the hood. He indulged in some dirt of his own, but had been fortunate enough to slip through the cracks—so far.

"You gotta stay out there."

"I know. I was out there chilling, cuz." Feeq said. He referred to him as his cousin because he messed with his little cousin. "This case is some old drug shit," Feeq said and shook his head.

"I got that shit for you."

Smitty reached inside his boxer briefs and pulled out a compressed bundle of weed and tobacco. Also buried inside the package were some Zanies.

Feeq dumped the pills and boosted his high with the weed daily to fly through the tedious hours of being down. The jail stayed locked down for stabbings or shortages of guards. The solitude could drive a nigga crazy, but the drugs took Feeq away from the reality of being trapped in the confines of cement walls and steel doors. He had a smartphone he'd paid Smitty to smuggle in for him, so he was comforted by hours of conversing and social media.

"I got this shit from Donnie. That little nigga out there pushing a Range now." Smitty was impressed with his upgrade. "And then, the he told me to call him Schemes now. I almost laughed in that nigga's face when he said that." They both chuckled.

"Yeah, they're out there eating," Feeq said, while reminiscing about the robbery they did together. "I gotta get back out there!" He rubbed his hands together with a devilish grin. "I gotta get back."

The money Feeq had was running dry. Between lawyer's fees, taking care of himself while down, and still trying to support wifey and the kids, he was being drained slowly but surely.

"Man, look at you. You talking about going right back at it as soon as you touch." Smitty was serious, but he was grinning at the same time. They both knew that, as soon as Feeq was on the other side of the fence, he would be right back at it. "Why don't you put me on some of that paper y'all be getting? I can move for you while you're down."

"Come on, Smitty. You know you ain't ready for that." He knew Smitty presumed that they hustled. He didn't know that they took money. Though he fell after the first job, Feeq kept in touch, so he knew they were still taking money. They were always fishing for a robbery.

"Ready for what? I'm ready for whatever, nigga." Smitty was trying to sound tougher than he was. Feeq knew Smitty more than he thought he did. He knew he was a chump from the hood who wanted to be looked at as if he was thorough. Smitty wasn't really a street dude, but, for some reason, he tried to be. Feeq knew he could manipulate him and use him for his own benefit while he was down. His money was damn near gone, so he considered using him as a puppet that he could use to pull the strings while he was down. Several more months and his pockets would be on E.

Feeq knew he could use Ghost, Schemes, and Reem as his pawns in his mental game of chess. He could put Smitty on to them to do a robbery and benefit from the proceeds.

"You're sure you're ready to get involved in this shit?" Feeq raised his eyebrows.

"Come on, man. It ain't no question. I'm trying to get all the way on. I just do this job to get by."

There was a moment of silence. "All right. Look..."

Feeq was interrupted by chatter and screaming coming from Smitty's walkie-talkie. While synchronizing, a lot of commotion could be heard outside the cell door.

Smitty barged out the cell, zoomed down the steps, and into the dayroom area. Feeq quickly tucked the package of drugs and 'bacco under his mattress and rushed out the cell to see what was going on. He was sure there was a rumble going on because he was very familiar with the sound of thumping and screeching feet on the ground.

Outside the cell, on the top tier, Feeq saw what looked like a rampage taking place in the common area. He cringed when he saw someone named Rico crack some other dude with a wooden floor brush. Blood instantly gushed from the dude's head after the brush created a wide-open gash. That didn't stop Rico from viciously whooping him with the floor brush. Rico ignored the blood coming from his own nose and continued to punish dude.

There were several other inmates going at one another at the same time. A man named Shiz, Rico's man, had a homemade shank tied to his hand with a piece of ripped bed sheet. He was going to work on another guy with a long piece of steel.

"Ah! Ah! Ah!" The dude let out a series of shrill cries as Shiz held him by his shirt for leverage and slammed the banger in and out him.

Feeq cringed over and over at the sight of the knife piercing dude's skin repeatedly. He even jumped and let out an "oh" as he watched the steel go in and out. There was too much commotion to watch the blood-shedding encounter taking place. There were, at least, four others trying to kill one another in the dayroom. Obviously, something had set off the war in the housing unit.

A stampede of correctional officers swarmed the block with their mace and handcuffs in hand. They stormed the brawl headfirst and seized them one inmate at a time.

"Everybody! To your cells! Everybody! Take it in! Let's go now!" the COs screamed in unison while banging the doors shut to secure the unit. Feeq stepped in his cell, followed by his celly, who slid in right behind him, just before the guard slammed and locked their door.

"Damn!" Feeq's celly said in excitement, "You see that shit?" Feeq stood at the door, peering through the thin Plexiglas. He ignored his celly's dumb-ass question. Of course, he'd seen it. The dayroom was a mess. Blood covered the floor, chairs, and tables. Cards and chess pieces had been knocked off the tables and were scattered everywhere. Nearly every cell had an inmate in the window, watching the others get escorted off the block in cuffs.

Feeq sighed with frustration.

"We stay locked down in this motherfucker," he said, complaining more to himself than his celly. He shook his head with disgust. "I gotta get the fuck outta here!"

CHAPTER 11

A couple of days went by, and Reem found out Toya was off from work on Sunday night, so they decided to run in the Walmart that night. It was perfect because not only was it holiday season, but the robbery was going down on Sunday after the big shopping weekend. Shoppers had more free time to spend their checks for the holidays on Friday and Saturday, so the store had to be loaded.

Reem, Schemes, and Ghost waited patiently in the dark, behind the department store. The area glowed a luminous orange because of the overhead night lights on the walls. The odor of garbage and stale urine polluted the air, captivating the robbers' nostrils.

Cloistered behind the dumpsters for cover, they had to remain steadfast until one of the employees emerged to bring out the trash. Frosty December air smacked against the revealed facial features from behind their masks. Ghost felt his lips getting crusty and kept licking them to temporarily sooth the irritation.

Patience was running thin because they had yet to see or even hear anyone approach the door. Crickets filled the silence, growing louder by the second, making the wait become more tense.

"Yo! What the fuck!" Ghost muttered at Reem. "You got us out here on the same dumb shit," he whispered, frustrated. He nudged his pistol with each word to emphasize his frustration before stuffing the gun back in his pocket. He was uncertain about the plan and was ready to abort the mission at any minute.

"Relax." Reem held his hand up, pumping it for Ghost to remain calm. "They're coming. Trust me," he said, but wasn't sure if he believed his own words.

Moments later, the clanking sound of a key unlocking the door echoed through the deserted area. They peaked at the rear door and watched as a male employee unlocked and came out the door. Reem looked at Ghost and shook his head with an *I told you so* grin on his face.

The employee dragged several bags and broken down cardboard boxes out. He leaned several boxes against the wall beside the door and carried two bags toward the dumpster. His hands were full, so running up on him would be sweet.

He would be caught off guard and would never have a chance to defend himself with his hands occupied. It was already agreed upon that Schemes would jump out to capture the employee when he came out. Schemes was bigger than the others, so it was best that he made the first move to exercise the advantage of his size. Schemes crouched down in a squatting position, prepared to lunge at his prey when he was within a good distance.

The employee was oblivious to the men behind the dumpsters. He whistled and bobbed his head as if tunes were playing between his temples. Just within a few feet of his grasp, Schemes was just about to make his leap at him but was startled by a loud female voice.

"You want some help out there, trash man?" the female employee joked with him from the doorway.

"Yeah. How about I throw your ass in this dumpster?"

The plan was sabotaged because of the unexpected female standing in the doorway. The male employee walked back over to get the other trash bags. He paused at the door, running his mouth with the chick. This gave them a little time to think, but only a few seconds because the man was making his second trip to the dumpster.

"Yo! Grab the dude. I got the bitch," Reem whispered as he inched to the edge of the dumpster.

"No." Ghost tried to stop him, but it was too late. Reem had already darted out in a full sprint toward the door with his burner pointed at the doorway.

Both employees were stuck in awe—the man because a flashing figure had suddenly burst past with what looked like a gun in his hand, and the woman because the dark figure was rushing toward her, pointing what she was sure was a gun at her.

The female's instinct kicked in a little too late, but soon enough to slam the door and crush the culprit's fingers in between it and the frame.

"Ahhh, shit!" Reem hollered in pain as his eyes nearly popped out of their sockets and grew to the size of Ping-Pong balls.

The woman's attempt to close and lock the door were thwarted by Reem's fingertips. With an aching hand, Reem fiercely ripped the door open, took the female by her collared shirt, and shoved his pistol in her face. Before she could make a plea for her life, she was airborne. Reem clipped her from behind with one leg and clotheslined her across the chest. She hit the ground quick and hard. He was on the verge of blacking out due to the anger as he raised his gun to strike her with it.

"Chill, dawg! What the fuck!" Ghost said from behind. He wrapped an arm around Reem. Then, he clutched his shoulder and pulled him back. "Come on, man. Stay focused." He tried to cool Reem off.

Schemes kept his .50 cal. Desert Eagle stuck to the male employee. The employee cooperated after the sight of the large weapon. They were certain they would use them, especially the angry one because he fiddled, gritted, and clenched his jawbone tight as if he was dying to pull the trigger to avenge his swollen finger.

"How many people are in here?" Ghost asked the male employee, putting his finger up to his mouth to let him know to answer quietly.

The man, obviously counting in his head, looked up at the ceiling as if he'd found the answer somewhere up there. Maybe he was saying a silent prayer asking to get out of this alive.

"Eight," he finally answered.

"Where are they located in the building?"

The man was growing impatient with the survey. He wanted desperately for this to be over, so he told them where he believed the other employees were.

They quickly bound the employees with zip-ties. They could tell they were in the warehouse of the store and quickly realized they had made a mistake. Although Reem knew where the manager's office was, he knew how to find it from the front of the store and not the back. They never got a full layout of the store and now had to find it. Before securing the two employees inside a smelly mop closet, they stripped them of their cell phones and found out how to find the manager's office. They told them both to stay in the mop closet without making a sound until they were discovered by someone else. The threat was understood, so they didn't mutter a sound.

Ghost, Reem, and Schemes crept through the warehouse with their guns drawn. From what the other employees told them they had an idea where to find the other employees and the office. According to them, there would be several workers doing stock and inventory in the warehouse and a couple more in the office.

Voices could be heard in the trenches of the dusty warehouse. They followed the voices, which grew louder the closer they got. Oblivious to the presence of the robbers, the employees were laughing and carrying on carelessly while taking inventory. They were equipped with scanners, clipboards, and other miscellaneous equipment.

They were caught off guard by the three masks who came up behind them from nowhere, swinging guns and making demands. They complied by dropping the equipment and falling to the ground, onto their bellies. They were stripped of their cell phones and tied up with zip-ties in a matter of seconds. Schemes towered over them while Ghost and Reem went to their final destination.

Ghost tapped on the manager's door after trying to twist the locked knob. Commotion could be heard from inside the office. Reem positioned himself on one side of the door while Ghost went to the other side, like they had been trained in a police academy.

"Didn't I tell you not to bother us?" a feisty manager said as he yanked the door open.

"Shut the fuck up!" Ghost snapped, shoving the gun in his face. Instead of finding one of his antagonizing employees, the manager was startled by men bursting through the door. His glasses were knocked from his face as he was swung to the floor.

A female employee was sitting on the other side of a table, counting money with a digital money-counting machine. In a matter of seconds, Ghost was around the table with her on the floor being hog-tied. Because they knew the manager was a guy, they turned their attention to him.

"Open the safe," Reem instructed, holding a .44 Bulldog at the back of his head. The Bulldog was anxious to bark at Reem's itchy finger holding the trigger.

The manger was whining like a little girl—literally. He was a full-blown gump. Everything but his manly features imitated a female. The way he spoke, the way he screamed, and his entire demeanor was that of a woman. Both Reem and Ghost pulled out black, large folded laundry bags from their waist sections.

"Open the fucking safe!" Reem repeated over the he-she's sobbing.

"I need my glasses," he managed to answer through sniffles.

Reem scanned the floor and handed him his cracked glasses.

Ghost was cleaning the money off the table while the man was entering the combination for the safe. When the safe cracked open, the sight was overwhelming—stacks of bills rested perfectly and safely inside. Well, at least, until they were being swept into the bag. The dead presidents weren't safe anymore as they were taken into the possession of the masked robbers.

After bagging all the currency, Reem tied the manager's hands and feet up. He giggled inside at the sight of the name tag pinned to the man's shirt: Ryan. And for a minute, he was worried about Toya wanting to stay at the job because she was fucking him. He had to smirk again at the thought of it. This time, he smiled openly, but no one but him knew why. It was his personal moment of self-amusement.

They locked the employees in the office and sped through the warehouse. Schemes followed them as they flew by him, carrying the large drawstring bags. Ghost smirked as he passed the mop closet where the other workers were still trapped.

Inside the stolen car, they disappeared into the darkness of the night, racing through the back blocks to the switch point. Then, they jumped into the Buick Century. As they flew down Michener Avenue, sirens could be heard screaming in the tranquil streets of Mount Airy. Someone must have finally gotten loose back at the store.

The ride back down the way was filled with adrenaline. With the trunk loaded with an underdetermined amount of cash, the take was back on. Laughter and excitement pervaded the car. Reem was just as excited, but they were laughing at him.

They were grinding him up about his bold move of running up on the female employee and getting his hand smashed in the door.

"Really funny, y'all! Real fucking funny!" he said, pulling the gloves off his hands and staring at his blood-clotted fingertips.

He thought, *That fucking bitch!*

CHAPTER 12

The Walmart jux was tallied at $378,000. This was somewhat expected. The split was tremendous. It was $125,000 a piece for less than five minutes of work. The only problem with the large lump sum was that there wasn't a secondary source of income since the war was still on.

The police were lurking, and they were sure Reese and Mar were still assembling a plan to touch the other side. Even though Ghost and his team were sitting on a nice piece of change, they still knew they had to strategize to get at Reese and Mar to put an end to the drama. Their whereabouts were just a mystery. They seemed to have vanished from the face of the earth.

The three of them took a little trip to Atlantic City to get away from the drama and have some fun. They needed desperately to enjoy themselves and splurge with some of the money they had come up on. Of course, Ghost and Reem had a lot of explaining to do to the women in their lives about the weekend they'd be missing in action. Over complaints, due to their insecurities, they accepted that their men wanted a little space.

"Snake eyes! All field bets a winner!" the casino employee yelled as the dice hit the wall of the crap table.

"Yo! It's jumping down here tonight," Reem said, walking up to the table where Schemes and Ghost were already stationed.

Well, Ghost was participating in the crap game while Schemes was in the ear of some woman. She looked like she was giving him some rhythm, too.

"Come on, nigga. This table is hot. Win some of the bread!" Ghost told Reem.

The Trump Casino was packed to the max, if it even had one. Drunk gamblers—men and women—played the games, chasing a few extra dollars. Of course, many left empty-handed or with dramatically less than what they had come with, all surging its way into the already overloaded pockets of the great Donald Trump.

Reem and Ghost were posted at the crap table, drinking and yelling along with many others surrounding the table's bar. Reem and Ghost's racks were aligned with hundred and twenty-five dollars chips. To them, they were the ballers at the table. Until, just like the previous night, a middle-aged man, clad in designer clothing, approached the table. With a complete rack of hundred dollar chips, the man threw his chips on the table and made his bets carelessly. He was betting thousands at a time, like money wasn't shit. Everything about him spelled money. The stud in his left ear twinkled off the light, saying, "We can hit the mall together." His *GQ* cover attire said, "Ain't nobody fresher." The Audemars Piquet watch wrapped around his wrist said, "You know what time it is!"

Dude knew all eyes were on him, too. People watched him with envious hearts and jealous stares. *Who is this dude?* Ghost wondered.

"Six hard! Six hard!" the casino employee yelled enthusiastically as a woman crashed the dice off the table's wall.

The payouts continued all night. The table was as hot as a pot of boiling water, so the gamblers' chips added up, bashing just a small dent in Trump's deep pockets.

Eventually, seven crept it's way on the table, cooling things down. Reem was past tipsy; he was pissy drunk, but Ghost was only buzzed from the few drinks he had thrown back. Schemes had spun off with the bunny he was rapping to. They probably were up in a room somewhere. Ghost and Reem had hit the food court to grab something to quiet their stomachs' rumbles.

"Yo! How much you win?" Reem asked with a slur.

"Don't count mine, nigga. Can't a nigga get money anymore?" They both laughed.

"Whatever, nigga," Reem retorted. "I know you came up something nice."

Ghost ignored Reem because he had the raps. He kept talking, but his words were going in one ear and out the other without registering at all. The liquor had him ramming incessantly. He was becoming a bit annoying, and Ghost wanted him to shut up.

Ghost's attention was diverted from his food to the figure hovering over his side. The man from the crap table approached.

"Y'all mind?" he asked, nodding his head toward the vacant seat at the table.

At first, they were reluctant to let him sit with them. They looked at each other with puzzled faces before telling him it was cool for him to take the seat. They didn't know who he was or what he wanted, but what harm could he do anyway? They were about to depart, calling it a night at any minute anyway.

"So how long y'all staying in town?" the man asked, breaking the ice.

"We're out of here tomorrow night," Ghost told him. "After we win a couple more dollars," he continued with a smirk.

"Yeah, we hit them hard tonight, didn't we?" the man said. "Better that than last night, huh?" Last night hadn't been so lucky.

"We never got your name," Ghost said.

"Oh, how rude of me. I'm Shareef." He held out his hand and gave both of them firm handshakes while maintaining eye contact. "I'm actually a good friend of your father's."

Ghost pulled back his extended hand. Before he or Reem could fully introduce themselves, the man made it known that he already knew who Ghost was. The mention of his dad was peculiar because he barely knew his own father, so who was this man, and how'd he know who his pop was?

The dialogue lasted awhile longer. Shareef told them how he and Ghost's dad were tight back in the day. He shared a few interesting stories that had them all cracking up. He explained how he had recognized Ghost the moment he saw him last night, but was hesitant to cut in on him, so he didn't say anything until he saw them eating at the table.

"So, I see y'all getting a little money. What y'all do for a living?" Shareef asked, indicating he had been watching them just as closely as they had watched him.

"We..."

Ghost started to speak but was interrupted by Reem.

"We take money," Reem recklessly blurted out.

Shareef furrowed his eyebrow at Reem's audacity and looked at Ghost to see if he would confirm what his man had just revealed.

"Listen. My man is a little drunk." Ghost looked at Reem with a *no you didn't just say that* frown on his face. "We run a little business of our own back home." He turned back to Shareef, knowing he wasn't buying the bullshit he'd just spit at him.

Shareef chuckled. He liked Ghost already for trying to clean up after his bonehead friend. Reem had allowed the alcohol to pass his judgment and give him loose lips. He had just revealed something that no one but their immediate circle should know to a complete stranger.

Ghost was furious with him. He could have knocked Reem out the chair he was sitting in. Luckily, Shareef wasn't a bad dude. He took a liking to Ghost, and he figured Reem wasn't too bad, either. He'd just let the liquor get the best of him. Little did they know, but they had more in common than they thought.

"So, what do you do?" Ghost asked, curious about where the old head was getting the paper he was flaunting.

Surprisingly, Shareef was upfront with them, but he had a little bit of sarcasm in his answer. "Well...ironically, I take money, too."

Reem had only been gone for a couple of days, but Toya was already missing the presence of her man. Only two days prior, he had departed for his gambling venture, and she was already yearning for his return. She missed the smooth sound of his voice, the way he spoiled her with gifts like every day was a holiday, and, most of all, the softness of his gentle touch. The way he held and looked at her demonstrated his love for her, so she knew he was falling in love with her, and she was falling even deeper for him. He was due home sometime today, and she couldn't wait.

"So tell me about this Mr. Wonderful you're dealing with," Rita said.

"Girl, where do I start? He's everything rolled into one. Just when I thought I couldn't love again, I fell for him," Toya said. "I've known him forever from around the way. I never thought we'd be fucking, but shit, since we've been getting it in, I can't get enough of him."

Rita sat quietly in the passenger seat. Even though she had started the conversation, she was now quiet. Toya wasn't sure if it was her jealousy or if she had drifted off to thinking about the robbery the other night at Walmart. Rita was the one who had slammed the door on one of the robbers' hands.

"Girl, why you get quiet all of a sudden?"

"I'm good. Just thinking," Rita said dismissively.

"Thinking about what? That shit that happened the other night?"

"Yeah, pretty much."

Rita didn't want to admit that she was a little jealous and envious of Toya because of her new relationship with Reem. Before she started messing with Reem, they would spend a lot of time together, but, since then, they weren't chilling together as much because she was always with her man.

Rita wasn't completely lying, though, because she was thinking about the robbery, too. One bad thing always triggers another, so she was thinking about how lonely she felt after being a victim of robbery.

"You'll be all right, girl," Toya said, rubbing her leg for comfort.

Rita nodded and mumbled, "That's easy for you to say."

Toya was one of the employees who was lucky enough to have had the horrific night off from work. Therefore, she didn't feel the pain of her friends. They were traumatized. Although she and Rita had talked about the event countless times, she still couldn't understand the wrath of her feet and hands stripped of their liberty.

"Girl, ya crazy ass slammed the door on that niggas's hand. Shit! At least, you put up a fight with your crazy ass." They both laughed about that.

Toya had initially questioned the black blood clots under Reem's nails to herself, but he had dismissed it as his hand getting slammed in the car door, so she thought it was a coincidence.

Rita told her about the time she spent in the mildew-infested mop closet. She shared the short-term memory that surfaced at the very smell of mildew. Toya was like her friend's personal shrink, listening and coaching her by day.

They were on their way to pick up their checks from the haunted Walmart. The December air was crisp but a bit warmer than usual. It was pushing sixty degrees outside.

Reem had finally laced Toya with a wheel. He got tired of taking her back and forth to work and damn near everywhere else she needed to go like he was her chauffeur. The fully-loaded Champagne 300C gleamed in the sun. Dr. Dre's Beats speakers rocked the interior of the car as Beyoncé boomed through the new line of speakers.

Toya loved her new car. She was sunk in the silky leather seat, gyrating to and singing the touching music. They whipped into the parking lot and parked in a vacant spot in the crowded lanes.

Nearly a week had elapsed, but Rita still became sullen at the sight of the store. She withdrew the second they entered the lot.

"Come on, girl. Let's go. It's all right." Toya rubbed her hand, trying to comfort her. She killed the engine, and they went inside the store. The last week at the gig was like walking in the center of an iceberg. The tension cut through the aisles of the department store like a fog driven cloud. People acted like the place was haunted or the robbers was coming back or something.

Today was no different. Rita was talking about quitting. Toya was there for her and let her know she had her support no matter what. Once Toya and Rita got their checks, they were on their way. The availability of a check-cashing place inside the store was convenient.

"You all right?" Toya asked.

"Yeah. I'm good, girl." Rita gave a dismissive wave, but she smiled an embracing smile to let her friend know she was good. Her mood lightened as they left the store.

Both women's heels clicked against the asphalt. Their hips swayed, letting others know they were more than some lousy department store employees. It was a life they didn't need, but they had come to love it.

They stood outside the Chrysler while Toya dug in her purse in search of her keys. A dark vehicle with MARTY'S PLUMBING on the side crept through the lanes of the parking lot, making its stop directly behind the Chrysler. The girls were oblivious to the tactic that they were being boxed in the parking spot.

"Y'all coming out?" a voice asked from behind the slightly lowered tinted window.

The van's occupant used the question to maneuver the van behind the Chrysler, leaving them with no way to back out of their parking spot.

"Yeah, we're coming out right now," Toya said, without looking up as she continued to rip through her purse for the keys.

Suddenly, the rear door of the van slid open, and two men with their faces covered jumped from the van's rear compartment. The dark blue bandannas covering their faces made the men look like violent Crips. They both held guns down by their sides and quickly bum-rushed Toya. They ignored Rita's presence. It was as if she didn't even exist.

Instantly, Toya screamed her lungs out of her chest. Rita's hollers emulated Toya's. The men ignored their screaming and grabbed Toya desperately to get her into the back of the van.

Toya wasn't surrendering without a fight. She punched one guy square in the center of his bandanna. She couldn't care less about the guns they were pointing at her. She knew, if they wanted her dead, she'd be gone by now. Besides, her instinct told her, if she allowed them to get her into the van, she'd be killed anyway. So she fought tooth and nail for the freedom attempting to be taken from her.

She wasn't alone either. Rita came from the other side of the car and started swinging on one of the dudes from behind. The one Rita griped and punched at ignored her frail hits and took Toya by her waist and lifted her off her feet. Toya's feet flailed in the air, and one caught the other dude in the chin.

The man stumbled back and grunted before gathering his composure. There was a clanking sound followed by a metallic scraping noise.

Fighting turned into sheer panic as the man dropped his gun. "Help!"

People started gathering around, but no one came to the aid of the women. They simply watched and scrambled on their cell phones, probably calling the police. The girls prayed that someone would help.

"Leave them poor girls alone!" someone shouted, but they weren't dumb enough to intervene physically.

The man who had gotten kicked in the chin dropped to his hands and knees and looked under the parked 300C where the gun had slid. He winced because the weapon was out of reach. He stood to his full six feet and boiled with rage.

"Let's get the fuck outta here!" the hidden face demanded from behind the wheel of the van.

The onlookers were growing, so they had to hurry up and get out of dodge.

The attempted kidnapper holding Toya gave up and slammed her forcefully to the ground, creating a loud thumping sound. Then, he turned around and sucker-punched Rita. He was sick of her punching him in the back of his damn head. The blow landed fiercely and made a crunching sound of knuckles against flesh. Rita fell flat on her butt.

"Fuck!" one of the men yelled in frustration as they retreated to the van.

After the rear door was shut, the van skidded in the same spot for several long seconds before the tire gripped the tarmac and screeched out the parking lot.

Toya and Rita laid between two parked cars, exhausted and terrified. Toya scooted her body under the car and grabbed the loaded pistol. She clenched it tight. She was sure, if she had had the gun moments ago, there would be flesh and blood decorating the parking lot.

The observers finally came forward to help and comfort them as whooping sirens grew louder and louder. An elderly man came forward and tried to take the gun out of Toya's hand.

"Give me the gun, dear," he said, crouching down by her side.

Reluctantly, Toya released the gun.

The threat was gone, but her quivering wouldn't stop as her nerves disobeyed her mind, telling her to calm down. She couldn't believe what had just happened.

"Do you know who those men were?" one of the people standing by asked.

Toya slowly shook her head.

"Who would try to hurt you, honey?" another voice asked.

Toya's shoulders lifted and dropped with an unsure shrug.

Her body language said she was in complete awe and confusion, but the look in her glimmering, raging eyes told a different story.

The men who tried to grab her were wearing bandannas, so, to the onlookers and overhead cameras, they were unidentifiable. But Toya stared into the eyes of the kidnappers, and, just then, she realized the shit she was stuck in the middle of. She had a good idea who the furious eyes hiding behind the bandannas belonged to.

Reese and Mar. It had to be.

CHAPTER 13

Ghost, Reem, and Schemes spent the last day in Atlantic City chasing Trump's paper. The money they'd won the previous nights had slowly been drained at the crap table.

Ghost and Reem introduced Shareef to Schemes, and the four of them took time out to get better acquainted before parting ways. They found out Shareef was only in the area for business. They all knew what that meant, but they refrained from questioning the old timer.

Reef now resided in Miami, but he was originally from Philly. He had taken his talents to South Beach. He was modest, but it was obvious he was living the life down there. He invited the crew to come down for a nice vacation, to get away from the hood, and enjoy themselves. They accepted the invitation and promised to keep in touch with him to set things up.

The ride home from Atlantic City was tedious in the afternoon traffic. Ghost drove while the others rested. Reem and Schemes were both out cold. Schemes was in the backseat, lying across the seat in the fetal position. He looked like a little boy on vacation with his parents. He even had his thumb in his mouth.

Reem was riding shotgun and was knocked out, too. He was leaning his head against the window and slobber was dripping down, dampening his Polo shirt.

They were in Schemes's Range Rover, and the heated seats were very relaxing. Biggie's *Life After Death* eased through the speakers, mellowing the ride with his vivid storytelling. Ghost turned the music down because, for the third time, he'd heard what sounded like an extra melody syncing with the beat.

He was right. Reem's phone was ringing off the hook. The soft Ne-Yo ringtone indicated it was Toya blowing him up. Ghost smacked Reem's shoulder to get him up.

"Yo! Answer your phone, dawg."

Reem mumbled something unintelligible, and Ghost smacked him again and said, "Man, answer your fucking phone! It's Toya, yo!"

"Fuck that bitch. I'll talk to her when we get home," Reem murmured. Reem must have been enjoying his rest because he would never brush Toya off like that.

Ghost was about to turn the music back up, but the annoying-ass ringtone went off again. This time, he smacked Reem on the cheek and shook him to get up.

"Man, answer your fucking phone or turn that shit off!" Reem slowly came out of his slumped state. He sucked his teeth, wiped the slobber from his chin, and rubbed it on his pants leg.

"Yeah," he said, answering the phone.

Immediately, Ghost knew something was wrong because Reem sat all the way up in his seat with an attentive look on his face. Ghost couldn't hear the other side of the conversation, but he didn't like what he was seeing from Reem's side.

"Stop crying," Reem said. "What!" he shouted. "Them niggas did what? Where...where you at?"

The conversation lasted several long minutes. Ghost kept glancing over at Reem, waiting impatiently for him to tell him something. Reem's concerned look quickly transformed into an angry frown. Ghost's instincts told him it had something to do with Reese. Things were quiet for too long. He wanted desperately for the whole thing to go away, but it just seemed like this shit would never end.

Ghost's suspicion was confirmed as soon as Reem hung up the phone.

"They tried to kidnap her, dawg," he said with tears in the confines of his eyes.

His glare was fixed on the windshield, but he wasn't looking at anything in front of him. He was painting a picture of Reese burning in hell. He vowed to himself that he was going to kill Reese and whoever else was behind the botched kidnapping.

Ghost was in his zone, too. He remembered the day he hit Reese up, and the gun jammed. He wished he would have died because now he was terrorizing their lives.

Only seconds of silence went by, but it felt like an eternity.

"Wake Schemes up," Ghost told Reem.

"Look at this fucking nigga!" He looked at Schemes curled up, sucking his finger. "Wake the fuck up, nigga!" he yelled, shaking him.

Schemes woke up angry.

"What the fuck, man!"

"Pussy, while you're back there sleep, Reese and them just tried to grab Toya!"

"What?" Schemes wasn't sure he was hearing things right. He blinked his eyes and rubbed them to make sure he was awake.

"Nigga, you heard what the fuck I said!"

"Why the fuck you snapping on me?" Schemes quickly defused the yelling.

They all sat in the car going on and on about how they were going to do Reese dirty. They snapped until they all fell silent. The only thing left to do was to get back to Philly, which couldn't happen fast enough.

The SUV raced through traffic on the crowded expressway. Ghost whipped the terrain vehicle lane to lane. The tires against the asphalt were the only sound ripping through the car as they sat speechless.

Up ahead, the road was full of red taillights as other cars sat, crammed in a traffic jam. Ghost stopped just before he hit the bumper of another car.

"Fuck!" he snapped, and he slammed on the horn. But nobody moved.

Back in Philly, Reese, Mar, and Reese's cousin, Terry, were sitting in the house. They were arguing in frustration, and couldn't believe Toya had fought avoiding capture. Shit had gone sour, and they were salty that they had had to abort the plan.

"I told you we shouldn't have done that shit in the parking lot like that!" Reese said at Mar.

"Where else were we going to find her, dickhead?" he insulted Reese, but they both knew it was the truth.

"Yo! Call me outta my name again!" Reese pointed his index finger at them.

Frustration had cluttered their thinking, so they were going at each other's necks. Terry tried to intervene, but they wouldn't listen. He was sick too because he was riding on the strength of his cousin, but didn't expect that these niggas couldn't even grab a bitch.

"Nigga, how the fuck you drop the gun?" Mar asked, taunting Reese.

"The bitch kept swinging her legs and kicked me in the face with those pointy-ass heels, and then she kicked the gun outta my hand," Reese explained. "Nigga, you had the bitch. Why the fuck you ain't pull her in the van?"

"Hold up! I know you ain't trying to blame me for that shit," Mar retorted.

Before Reese could say anything else, Terry butted in, "Come on, man. Y'all arguing over nothing. We gotta find another way to touch them," he said, making sense.

"I feel you, but this dickhead—"

Mar's insult was cut short as Reese jumped from the couch and went trucking for Mar like Damarcus Ware sacking his rival Eli Manning.

The two of them crashed into and crumbled the coffee table in the center of the living room. They wrestled and swung at each other nonstop. After failing to pry them off one another, Terry plopped down on the sofa and smirked. He sat there, watching them tussle. He knew that, eventually, they would get enough, but, first, they needed to relieve their frustration and embarrassment. They needed to take it out on somebody, so why not one another? Terry winced at a sucker punch Reese caught Mar with and just shook his head.

The next day seemed like it took forever to roll around. Once back in Philly, Ghost and his crew spent the remainder of the day and night looking for Reese and Mar. Though Toya thought it was them, she wasn't positive, but they knew it had to be them. They learned from Toya that there was another person involved, but she said that he had stayed in the van. They had no clue who the dude could have been, but whoever he was, they promised themselves they'd bury him next to the other two.

They combed the hood looking for Reese and his acquaintances. They asked everyone they knew about any possible whereabouts, and, unsurprisingly, no one had any idea where they were laying low at. People in the hood were actually shocked to see Ghost and them in the hood. They knew bloodshed was soon to be poured.

They were all introduced to Rita. Rita was still a little shaken up, not only by the Walmart robbery, but now the attempted abduction of her best friend was adding to the tragic chain of events. What Rita didn't know was that the men who took the Walmart down had been sitting right next to her for the last couple of days. Toya had kept Rita up under her wing over the last few days to comfort her. Truthfully, Toya needed her friend's comfort because she was shaken up, as well.

Ghost was on the phone with Shareef, filling him in on everything that had taken place. He needed someone to vent to, and, though he didn't know Shareef that well, it gave him someone to talk to. He could talk to someone else, but, they were all heated and wouldn't serve as much help.

Ghost only intended to tell the old head about the kidnapping attempt, but Shareef wanted to know everything, so Ghost explained how everything had transpired from the pistol-whipping of Reese to the attempted abduction of Toya.

Because Shareef was an old-timer, he gave some good advice and suggestions. Ghost had never had a close relationship with his father; therefore, he had never really had much of a male mentor, but, for some reason, Shareef had filled that void since they met.

"Sounds like you have your hands full, young fellow," Shareef said, a bit concerned.

"Yeah, but we'll catch up with those dudes sooner or later."

"What if he catches up with you first?" Shareef caught him off guard with the question.

Though the question was real and had some base to it, Ghost didn't like the sound of it. He felt his temper boiling and rising, ready to erupt at any second.

"What? That pussy can't touch me! I'm gonna crush that nigga on sight!"

More steam built up inside Ghost when Shareef audaciously laughed at him. He didn't think shit was funny, yet Shareef obviously did on the other side of the phone.

"What the fuck is funny, man?" he asked, as he started to lose it a little.

Reef sensed the youngin's temper flaring and said, "Calm down, little man." Then, he checked him. "I'm on your side here, but let me tell you something. The art of war is 'don't start a war,'" Shareef added seriously with all traces of humor erased from his tone.

Ghost took the phone from his ear and looked at it with his face balled up. *Who this nigga think he is?* he asked himself.

Shareef continued his lecture. "It's too late for that now though because y'all have a war on y'all hands, so now you have to figure out how to come out on top. Don't ever underestimate your opponent, especially after they show that they're willing to go the distance with you. You can be touched, too, Ghost. Never forget that."

"Man, that pussy tried to kidnap my man's bitch and couldn't even do that right, so how he going to get at me?" He was heated and not thinking straight. "That was some bitch shit he did!"

"Ha! See, that's where you are wrong. There's only one rule to war, and that's to win." Shareef dropped a jewel on him. "They're trying to win, are you?" he asked but wasn't really looking for an answer.

"Oh, I'ma win all right!"

"Listen, will you? They say a hard head makes a soft ass, and that's where you're going to end up—on your ass if you don't get outta your feelings."

"Feelings?" Ghost said sarcastically. "I ain't no emotional nigga!"

"Yeah? Well, let me tell you this. A war is fought with fifty percent heart, twenty-five percent mind, and twenty-five percent ability. Both of you have showed some heart, but you know what they showed that you all haven't?" he asked, knowing Ghost wouldn't know the answer.

"What?"

"Mind. They have showed they're using their heads to get at y'all. While you are bullshitting in AC, they're trying to snatch Reem's girl. Now, their ability to execute was a little fucked up," Shareef said, chuckling before continuing, "but, right now, you're not using your head. I don't know about Reem and Schemes, but you are acting off emotions right now, so your judgment is clouded. I can't believe you right now, but I know, if you don't pull yourself together, you're going to get killed."

He was starting to make a lot of sense to Ghost. The conversation lasted another fifteen minutes before he offered for Ghost to bring his family and friends down to Miami for a minute.

"I don't know, man. I have a lot on my plate, and I have to put an end to this shit once and for all," Ghost told him in response to the invitation. "I ain't running from these niggas."

"See, there you go again. You're not using your head. You're thinking with your heart. We both already know you got heart, but you have to use your head. Come on down and clear your head, and let me think of a way to help you, all right?"

After a brief moment of silence, Ghost agreed. "All right, old head, but we have to end this shit ASAP."

"Ghost, they can't touch what's not there. There is always a reason for what I say, so get packed up, and I'll have arrangements made for a private jet to fly you guys down."

"You own a jet?" Ghost asked, shifting the subject.

Shareef laughed and said, "I wish! Naw, man. I have a membership with NetJets. You'll love it, so quit the questions and round the fam up. I'll call you back with the time and all for the flight."

Ghost was digging his pop's friend. He was looking forward to getting more acquainted with him. He went to start packing his bags. He had a flight to catch.

They can't touch what's not here, he thought.

CHAPTER 14

It wasn't hard to convince the others to take the trip down Miami. They were sure that there would be sunnier days in the city of partying and bullshit.

The seven of them boarded the private jet in amazement. None of them had ever experienced such luxury before. The interior was astounding. Marble tables complimented the milky butterscotch seats and cream carpet. They got comfortable quickly, watching television on the screens mounted above the seat.

They even dragged Frog along with them for the getaway to keep him settled and out the streets for a while. Rita found a way to squeeze herself into the plans of the sudden visit down south. Kia's brother Bird kept Khashan with him while they went away.

The amenities the flight attendants provided were comforting. Ghost drifted off in thoughts about how the money he had was nothing compared to the life Shareef was living. He estimated that an annual membership with NetJets would cost his entire stash alone.

Frog was stuck in a reverie of his own. Staring at the vacant seat, he thought about his best friend Snook and how he should be there with them. He grimaced and vowed to kill those responsible or join his homie in the dirt. Street justice still hadn't been exercised on Reese and his team, and he felt like they were running from their problems. He wasn't feeling the shit Ghost was kicking about using their heads and niggas couldn't touch what they couldn't feel. He agreed to take the trip but promised himself he would move with or without them.

When the flight landed, a stretch limo was awaiting their arrival to transport them to their destination. According to Reef, their hotel reservations had already been made.

"Damn! This shit is nice," Kia said, loving the scenery.

"Yeah, I can't wait to get out on these streets and get at some of these chickens," Schemes said.

"That's all you think about. Your dick is going to fall off!" Kia said seriously, but laughed afterward.

Reem was the only one who peeped Rita roll her eyes. She tried hard to hide the jealousy, but she wasn't doing a good job at it. Reem knew she was feeling Schemes, and Schemes probably knew, too, but didn't give her much rhythm.

The limo driver had strict instructions to take them straight to their hotel, so they could get comfortable. Aligned in the back of the limo, they wasted no time popping a few bottles of champagne and filling flutes with drinks they'd never even heard of. Who cared? They were in Miami, so they popped the corks and guzzled the contents.

"Damn! Slow down, Schemes," Ghost told him.

Schemes didn't bother filling a flute with the drinks. He drunk straight from the bottle.

"I'm here to ball out!"

Another eye roll from Rita. Toya caught this one, though.

"Girl, let me find out," she said, nudging Rita with her arm.

"Find out what?" Rita's smile covered her whole face.

Only Reem knew what they were talking about because he could tell she was feeling his man.

As soon as the plane landed, they forgot what they were in the city for. The purpose of them coming down south was to escape the madness taking place back at home. Shareef's suggestion was to come down to Miami to get away from Philly for a while. He wanted to devise a plan to put an end to Ghost's problems.

Shareef wasn't a killer, though he was willing to. However, he was more of a thinker. One who could devise a plan to take over the world. He had plans to put Ghost on to some major money, but, with the drama taking place, he knew it wasn't a good idea to mix the two.

Frog rolled down the window and the southern heat instantly smacked them in the face.

"Damn! you see that Lambo?" he said with his arm out the window, pointing at a black Lamborghini that was passing in the opposite lane.

Schemes tugged at his shirt. "Man, act like you been somewhere before! You look like a groupie—all pointing out the window and shit!"

Everyone in the car burst into laughter. Frog smirked as well. He knew he was out of line for pointing like a fan seeing their favorite music artist.

"Whatever. That's going to be me one day," Frog said with certainty.

"Oh, yeah, and how the hell are you going to get that?" Schemes asked.

All eyes were on Frog. He was dead serious, and the look on his face showed it. He had no doubt in his mind that he would, one day, be a rich man.

"I'ma take it!" he told them with a sly grin.

Back in Philly, between the confines of the brick layered CFCF, Feeq was roaming the corridors of the county jail. He was fortunate enough to recently gain a job in the receiving room, so he was able to move throughout the jail. It was better than being booked in a cell for countless hours.

While in the hall, he saw Rico being escorted down the hall by an officer. Rico was draped in an oversized orange jumpsuit with his hands handcuffed behind his back.

"Step against the wall for me," the guard instructed Feeq, while holding Rico by the arm.

It was procedure for the officers to secure the inmates who were handcuffed while in the presence of other inmates who were unsecured, so the guard made Feeq stay against the wall within a safe distance from Rico while he escorted him from the hole to the visiting room.

"What's good?" Feeq asked Rico as he was passing by.

"Ain't shit. They gave me ninety days in the twist for that shit," Rico told him, wearing a smirk. He was obviously proud of the work he'd put in. "Send me some grub down and something to read."

"I got you," Feeq promised. Feeq was very familiar with doing time in the hole, so he knew how rough it could be.

"Don't send me no bullshit, like all those hood novels that be the same about how niggas be kingpins and all that," Rico said.

"I got you. I'ma send you *Corrupt City* by Tra Verdejo and *Project Terror* by Jamal Lewis. They're urban, but they're on some different shit. They're hot!"

"Who?" Rico asked, unfamiliar with the titles. He was just entering the visiting room.

"Man, I got you!" Feeq shouted, so he could hear him as he disappeared behind the door.

When Feeq arrived at the receiving room, Smitty greeted him as soon as he was buzzed through the door. Smitty was assigned to duty in the overcrowded intake room that day. He was slumped in the chair, blowing on the phone, getting paid for exactly what correctional officers did—nothing.

"What's good?" Smitty asked Feeq, hanging up the phone.

"Ain't shit." Feeq lifted himself over the counter to see the platter in front of Smitty. "I see you're eating good."

"Yeah, if you wanna call this eating good." Smitty downplayed the grub which was mouthwatering. "I'm trying to eat like you, playa. You ain't forgot me, did you?"

"Naw, I'm a hit up my neph and see what I can put together. I haven't spoken to him in a few days." Smitty reminded him that he could manipulate Schemes into doing a robbery with Smitty and breaking bread with him. "As a matter of fact, let me use one of the phones down here," Feeq continued.

"Go ahead."

Feeq stepped off to go use the institutional phone in the receiving room. He knew he should have waited until he got back to his cell to use the cell phone, but he was just as anxious to make the call as Smitty was. Little did he know, they both were trying to use one another for their own personal gain.

Feeq dialed the number and heard Schemes pick up. Next, he waited for him to accept the call.

The entire entourage finally reached their hotel in Miami. They all departed to their separate rooms. Ghost and Kia shared a room, and Reem and Toya had one of their own as well. Everyone else had personal rooms for the stay.

The evening was winding down, so everyone agreed to lie back for the night. They planned to hit the streets the next day to ball out. Ghost had plans to meet up with Reef the next day.

Instead of being cooped up inside the dry-ass hotel rooms, they agreed to meet at the outdoor pool. The seven of them were spread out around the pool area, which was packed with others.

Ghost and Kia were in the pool intimately cuddled. Ghost rested his back against the ledge of the pool while Kia straddled her legs around his waist. Things were beginning to heat up between the two of them.

Reem and Toya weren't doing anything much different. They, also, occupied the far end of the pool's corner, indulging in some passionate kissing, fondling, and whispering. Toya was sinking herself deeper and deeper into his heart. She had yet to admit it, but Reem had already locked in a place of her heart. She just had some skeletons in her closet that she hadn't yet revealed. She planned on telling him during this getaway, but she was waiting for the perfect moment to present itself.

Meanwhile, while other hotel stragglers frequented the pool area, Schemes found himself getting acquainted with a half-drunken Rita. They were slouched back in beach chairs, conversing.

"I needed this getaway," Rita vented. "It has been a long week for me."

"Shit! You ain't the only one, baby girl," Schemes concurred. "Child, let me tell you. Someone robbed the Walmart while I was working. They tied me up and put me in a damn mop closet for I don't know how long. Then, some nigga tried to kidnap Toya. I wasn't having that though."

Schemes swallowed hard at the mention of the Walmart robbery. While he was a bit nervous that Rita would pick up on his guilty demeanor, he was, also, cracking up inside because she didn't even realize she was sitting right next to one of the people that had held the store up.

Schemes was starting to dig Rita. She was thorough all the way around the board. She wasn't the prettiest, but she wasn't the ugliest either. On a scale from one to ten, Schemes rated her at about a seven or maybe an eight. He could tell she was intelligent because she had a lot of knowledge, ranging from sports to politics. They conversed about nearly everything.

Though Rita was a bit tipsy, she peeped how Schemes was studying her. His eyes could burn holes in her. She was coated with a brown texture, which was enriched with a glossy glow. The length of her hair couldn't be determined because it had extensions in it, which made her hair slither down past her shoulders. Her fingers and toenails were freshly done as well. But what was grasping Schemes's attention was her body in her bikini. She was petite but with curves, a flat stomach, eye- catching hips and a perky ass. A perfectly round set of D-cups rested steady inside her top without sagging.

Rita definitely had Schemes's attention because not far from where they were sitting, Frog was chilling with not one but two bad woman.

Schemes planned to hit as many chicks as he could while down in Miami, but, so far, Rita had him distracted.

"Rita, you know what? I'm really digging—"

Schemes was interrupted by his phone ringing. The display screen told him it was his uncle calling. A quick thought about how much his uncle was missing while locked up passed through his head while listening to the automated machine.

"Yo, unc!" he said, accepting the call.

"What's good, neph? My bad. I haven't hit you in a minute." Schemes knew his uncle well enough to know by that lousy statement that Feeq needed something.

They went through the motions, engaging in a bunch of small talk. Feeq was excited to hear they were in Miami. He asked who Shareef was but brushed it off once he learned he was a friend of Ghost's pop.

"Hey! Yo, things are getting dark for me, neph." Feeq paused to allow the hint to sink in and then added, "I need you to get with Smitty."

"Smitty?" Schemes didn't recognize the name.

"Oh, my bad, D. We call him Smitty in here. The one who messes with—"

"Yeah, yeah, I know who you're talking about. I just saw him like a week ago," Schemes interrupted.

"Yeah, I know. I heard y'all are doing it big out there, too. But listen, I need you to get with him ASAP, so y'all can put something together," he said, hoping his nephew caught on to what he was saying without him having to go into detail over the institutional phone.

"Put something together? Come on, unc. I don't even know dude like that." Schemes couldn't believe he had asked him to do something with someone he barely knew. He knew Feeq was talking about doing a robbery with Smitty, but he wasn't with it. Just because he messed with his cousin Taniesha, he really didn't want to move with him because he didn't really know him. On top of that, the nigga was a CO. He wasn't a cop, but shit, he was the closest thing to it.

The call lasted several more minutes. Feeq was persistent in trying to convince Schemes that Smitty was good people and could be trusted. Schemes was glad when the automated female told them the call was moments from being disconnected. His uncle was spoiling his mood, but, when he hung up, he decided that he wasn't going to allow it to ruin his night.

"What's wrong?" Rita asked.

She had heard the whole conversation. Well, at least, Schemes's side, but she tried not to be too nosy. Sensing his uneasiness, she became physical, trying to comfort him. She sat on his lap and the two of them locked eyes, talked, laughed and drifted off in their own little world. Stuck in their mingling, Schemes couldn't help but think about how down to earth Rita was. A flashback played in his head: the night Reem clotheslined her and she hit the ground like she was in the ring with Hulk Hogan. The thought almost made him laugh in her face.

He was snapped back to reality when Frog slid by with the two dime chicks he was chilling with trailing behind. As he passed, he winked at Schemes and said, "I'll holler at you tomorrow, playboy."

Frog wore an ear to ear smile. One of the chicks cut her eye at Schemes as she passed.

Damn! Schemes thought.

CHAPTER 15

Ghost had canceled the meeting with Shareef the night before because things had heated up between him and Kia. It didn't take long before they found themselves heading from the pool back upstairs to their room. The Miami atmosphere had a way of setting the mood for steamy sex.

Today, Ghost was rolling with Shareef. Much to his surprise, Shareef picked him up in a Maybach 62. They played the back of the Bach while a personal driver rolled them through South Beach. Ghost kept his composure, but he couldn't believe he was riding in a Maybach. Just several months ago, he was stuck in a building with dreams of riding in the cars he watched rap stars in videos ride in. Now, he was slouched in the snow-white machine and was enjoying every second of it.

Not only was the car immaculate, but the city was a sight to see—palm trees, expensive cars, and half-naked women walking the streets like it was normal. Ghost noticed he was the only one who seemed to be amazed. Everyone but him was used to seeing what he was just now seeing. He was running late.

"I see you like it down here, huh?" Shareef asked, noticing Ghost's eyes glued outside the window.

"Like it? I love it!" he answered. Ever since the moment he touched down in South Beach, his head was on a swivel, taking in the sights.

"You'll have plenty of time to enjoy yourself. But right now let's talk about what you came down here for."

The thought of Reese had yet to cross Ghost's mind since the departure of the private jet. At the moment, all he thought about was money and women and cars and clothes.

"Damn, did you see that chick right there?" Ghost said, nearly breaking his neck.

"Do me a favor. Pull that curtain shut, Ghost." Shareef's patience was at its thinnest.

He liked Ghost, but his lack of attention and seriousness bothered him. Here it was, they had an urgent matter on their hands, and Ghost seemed to have little to no concern about it. Ghost reluctantly drew the curtain in the Maybach's window closed and gave Shareef an irritated look.

"Ghost, you got people that want you dead, and here you are worrying about these bitches out here! You will have plenty of time to worry about that, but, right now, we need to talk about how to handle this situation you got yourself in!"

Ghost remained silent for a second before saying, "You're right." He knew Shareef had invited him and his family down to his city to get away and figure things out. He felt bad because Shareef was embracing him and his family. Their problems came along with them and he accepted that as well. Reef obviously wasn't playing, and it was time for him to take him more seriously. But he figured a little fun while miles away wouldn't hurt. But Shareef was right about them having plenty of time for that later.

"So tell me about these dudes you're at it with." Reef broke the silence first.

Ghost filled him in on everything he knew about them and ran the whole thing down to him about how the drama began in the first place. But something really stood out to Shareef and he couldn't believe they hadn't picked up on it yet.

"You mean to tell me this nigga's mom rests her head on the block y'all hustle on?"

Ghost knew instantly where he was going with things. He could have smacked himself in the forehead for being so dumb. A million scenarios popped in his head instantly.

"But Lindell is a fiend. He doesn't give a fuck about her."

"Any nigga that doesn't give a damn about his mother is coldhearted."

"Yeah," Ghost agreed.

"It's only one way to find out."

More silence. It was understood that Lindell was the key to getting at Reese. Ghost wanted to have some fun while away, though.

"Yo! This wheel is crazy!" Ghost complimented the Maybach. "You want one?" Reef asked nonchalantly, as if the car was nothing.

"Huh?" Ghost murmured, his eyebrows shooting up, wrinkling his forehead. He didn't think he'd heard him right.

Reef couldn't help but chuckle. "You're in Miami, baby boy. You can rent one of these down here for a few grand a day."

"Oh, this is a rental?"

"Oh no, baby boy. This here is mine. I put in a lot of work for this here. But you can rent all types of cars down here. Shit! You would never imagine. How much paper you bring down with you?"

"Something light."

"Something light, huh?" Another chuckle. "Well, before the day is out, I'll take y'all to the spot to lace you and your peoples." Ghost simply nodded. He was looking forward to getting behind the wheel of something exotic. The trip to Miami wasn't a bad idea after all.

The rest of the entourage met in the hotel's eatery to enjoy lunch together. Breakfast had been served courtesy of room service.

Schemes pulled his seat up next to Rita's. The previous night he wasn't sure if Rita was playing hard to get or if she had morals because she refused to go to the room with him after the numerous advances he had made. He had kicked all the game in the world, trying to get her to bite, but she wasn't going for it despite being tipsy.

Her standards only attracted him more to her. Maybe that was her intentions to begin with. Knowing that if she would have given it up too quick and easy, she would have defeated what she stood for, and he would've ran right off to the next piece of pussy.

They missed Ghost's presence. They knew he was with Shareef somewhere. Kia and Frog had been up when he left the hotel in the morning. The both of them were stunned when the Maybach pulled up. Ghost had looked like a kid climbing into the huge car.

"Ghost called and said he was taking us to rent some cars, y'all," Kia told the rest of them.

That excited everyone. They couldn't wait to get out and enjoy the city. They all knew they were there to stay away from Philly for a second, but they wanted to ball out while they were down south.

Frog had had the time of his life last night. He learned the two woman he was with the night before were from Chicago. They were shy at first, but afterward they explored one another's bodies—bi-curiously. *What happens in South Beach stays in South Beach*, he thought. Eventually, the Florida sun eased through the shades, awakening them. As if on cue, Frog kicked the two freaks right out. They seemed just as eager to go as he was for them to roll. Not looking for much more themselves, the hoes quickly gathered their scattered belongings and vanished.

Toya and Reem were seated by one another at the table. Reem was so busy digging in his chicken alfredo dish, he didn't notice Toya's attention diverted across the table. However, although Schemes was mingling with Rita, he peeped Toya constantly cutting her eye at him. The two of them were laughing, whispering, and all into one another. Between bites, Toya would steal a glance across the table.

Schemes's intuition picked up on her looks, telling him Toya was feeling him. He wondered if Reem or Rita had picked up on her wandering eye, but he appeared to be the only one to see it. He even locked eyes with her a couple times, which meant she wasn't hiding her looks. He couldn't help but wonder why she was checking him out the way she was. Did Reem have a bad girl? An untraceable smile formed, and he wondered if it was visible to anyone else or was the grinning all inside his egotistical mind.

Later that evening, the girls were out on the road enjoying life. Although Kia barely knew Rita and Toya, she decided to spend the night out with them to have a little fun. The men could use the space while the girls got better acquainted.

They rolled down Ocean Drive in a hot pink Lamborghini Aventador. Earlier, Ghost had taken them all to get rental cars to enjoy the luxury of the south. Kia had rented a McLaren, but she'd left the coupe parked at the hotel in order to ride with the girls.

The sun crept lower and lower, and the blazing temperature went with it. The sky was orange, and the air was crisp with a light humidity. The evening was just right as drivers filled the streets in all sorts of expensive wheels and as pedestrians covered the sidewalks.

People were half-dressed. Kia and the girls weren't wearing much of anything themselves. Kia had squeezed into some skin tight Seven jeans, and her belly, back, and shoulders were revealed because of the bikini top she wore. Toya was behind the wheel of the Lambo. Rita played the passenger seat while Kia worked the ledge in between the seats.

The three of them were gone off the countless drinks they'd guzzled all day. If the police got behind them, Toya would be visiting the gray-bar hotel for driving under the influence. But that would be the case for many of the tourists because everyone seemed to be on.

Rita couldn't sit still in her seat. She was constantly standing up or resting her ass on the headrest where the next person in the rental would be resting their head.

The Lambo drifted down the block. The eye-catching pink car caught the attention of nearly everybody out. It was definitely a head turner. Nicki Minaj's *Pink Friday* blasted through the custom speakers and had people dancing to the music.

Two men walking together on the sidewalk had their gazes fixed on the chicks in the Lambo. Rita locked eyes with them, shifting back and forth from one to the other. The men were clad in nothing but shorts and sandals, showing off their bodies. They were both tall brothers with pecs bursting from under their chocolate skin. Their bodies were completed with broad shoulders and flawless abs.

The girls were several cars back, stopped at the traffic light. The fellows came straight at them.

"Damn! Can we roll wit y'all?" one of them asked from the crowded pavement.

Toya and Rita were flattered, but Kia tried to act like she didn't hear them. Rita didn't have no shame in her game. The drinks had her on. She stooped up in the seat and started dancing to the music. Her skirt was hiked up, revealing her ass cheeks, and she didn't even bother to pull it back down.

"Damn, baby girl!" one of them said.

"What's up with y'all?" the other asked.

Toya turned down the music to give them a little play.

"What y'all getting into?" one of them cracked.

"Ain't shit. We down here just having a little fun," Toya said. "I see, y'all tryna get together? We got a suite with a Jacuzzi and all," one of the buffs said, trying to lure them.

"Yeah?" Rita asked, acting interested. "Too bad we don't do the dick thing. I mean, y'all are sexy and all, but I don't think my girl here would like it if someone else touched me," Rita continued.

"Oh, that's how y'all get down?"

Rita let actions answer that. She leaned over and grabbed the nape of Toya's neck. Then, she kissed her smack on the lips. Toya invited the embrace, and the two of them tongue wrestled for several seconds before coming up for air.

Kia's eyes shot open in amazement. She was caught off guard just as much as the dudes were, but she said nothing. One of the men rubbed Rita's ass while she was bending over kissing Toya. She smacked his hand away and said, "Look, but don't touch!"

The light up ahead turned green, and traffic slowly pulled off. Toya turned the music back up. As the car started inching away, Rita slid her skirt all the way up and started clapping her ass to the beat. Nicki Minaj and Sean Garrett's "Massive Attack" came blasting through the speakers. The hook of the song echoed down the block. Every time Sean Garrett made his gun sound effect, "blah, blah, blah," Rita made her ass clap in sync.

THE TAKE

The two dudes stared, smiled, and shook their heads as the car full of freaks slid off.

CHAPTER 16

Ghost sank into the smooth leather of the Maybach 62. The rental made him feel like he was a little boy again. He was as excited as a child on Christmas morning. His slim frame was swallowed by the spacious interior. Unlike Shareef, he wanted to push himself, so he didn't get a personal driver. The car vibrated with Meek Mill's, *I'm A Boss*, which featured Rick Ross as it slithered down Ocean Drive.

In front of Ghost, Reem was leading the way in a black Lambo. The others followed Reem as they headed to the club. Frog was behind Ghost in a Ferrari, and Schemes pulled up the rear in a Rolls Royce.

Ghost wore a sly grin as they made their way through town. The feeling was indescribable. It was like living in a music video. He remembered the days he was down and in jail. Now, he had returned to the top of his game in only a few months. All thanks to the take. Heads turned as the line of flashy wheels pulled up to the club. They hopped out, and, just like everyone else at the scene, they rocked designer clothing and shoes. Valet parking was also lined with all types of expensive cars. Women were in numbers, and many of them stood around mingling with one another and the ballers who were out for the night. It looked like the entire city had shown up.

Everyone at the party looked like they were getting money, and the woman were all dimes. Bottles were being popped all night. Ghost watched as a waitress flew by with a bottle on top of a tray. The bottle had sparkles flying from it, lighting up the club. It was undoubtedly the most expensive bottle in the house. All eyes followed the bottle to its destination, a corner in VIP where a group of men were sitting with a flock of women surrounding them.

Bottles of their own cluttered Ghost's entourage table. He wanted to order one of the sparkling bottles once he saw it, but didn't want to make it seem like he was competing with some niggas he didn't even know.

Women surrounded Ghost and his friends at their table as well.

"So, what's up? Can I roll with you tonight?" an attractive woman asked Ghost.

Though Ghost was faithful and loyal to Kia, the chick straddling his lap was bringing on one hell of a temptation. As her curves sank into his lap, the liquor played a big part in his manhood bulging from his pants.

"I don't know, baby girl. I got a girl," Ghost told her, regretting the words as they left his mouth.

"A girl? Shit! I got a man." The girl's eyes scanned the club. "I don't see either of them in here," she added convincingly. She had a point, too. "I won't tell if you won't tell." She rubbed his chest up and down with her index finger. She was very persuasive.

Ghost thought about how easy it would be to check into a separate hotel, crush this freak out, clean up, and head back to the hotel with wifey. Kia would never suspect a thing. Just as the thought started winning in his head, his phone rang. The screen told him it was Shareef. He'd been awaiting his call.

"I have to take this, baby girl." She sucked her teeth as she scooted off him.

"Yo, Reef!" He answered the phone while stepping inside the bathroom to drown out the music.

"Where you at, baby boy? It sounds like you're partying."
"Yeah, I was waiting on you."

"All right, I need to see you in person. So what time can you meet me back at the telly?" Reef asked.

"I'm on your watch, OG."

"What time are you leaving the club?"

"I can leave now. I'll be there in less than a half if you're ready for me."

"Perfect. I'll be there in twenty minutes." Reef loved the sense of urgency Ghost had. He was obviously clubbing, but he was ready to leave at the drop of a dime.

Ghost informed the others that he was rolling out. They were so caught up with the ladies at the table that they didn't even ask Ghost where he was going. The chick Ghost was kicking it with was more worried about his departure than them. She stared at him through lustful eyes as he gave daps to his boys. He left without saying goodbye to her.

She was left there with her mouth dangling wide open. *Fuck her! She'll find another nigga soon as I leave*, Ghost thought. He was right. Before he even got out the door, she was on to the next one.

As the night wore away, Frog became a bit irritating from the alcohol. His already throaty voice got louder and louder and carried throughout the club. Not long after Ghost left, Reem made his way back to the telly. He was on and horny and wanted to get up in something. Schemes was left with his cousin

Frog. They convinced some chicks to go back to the hotel with them, but, before they could get out the club, all hell broke loose.

Frog, staggering, bumped into another dude not far from the doorway.

"Yo! Look the fuck out!" Frog snapped on buddy.

All Frog had to do was say *excuse me* and keep it moving, but the drinks had him in his bag. "Man, watch where the fuck you're going," dude barked back with a hint of a southern accent.

Without any more rap, Frog threw a combo of wild punches, crashing against dude's jaw and midsection. Frog was always on go-time. The two of them wrestled and swung recklessly at each other. Schemes tried hard to pry the two apart. Frog always got into something no matter where they were. Now, Schemes regretted being left alone with his little cousin. He had no choice but to start pummeling the guy with Frog.

Commotion broke out inside the club. Two buffs with black T-shirts with SECURITY written across them were sliding through the crowd.

They grabbed Schemes and Frog but left the other one unattended. Somehow, Frog squirmed and wiggled out the hold the bouncer had him in. He pushed the bouncer in the chest, but he didn't even move a foot backward from Frog's weak shove. The security was husky, 6'3" and, at least, a solid 240 pounds with muscles busting out of his tight-ass shirt.

"Get the fuck off me!" Frog yelled.

A slight smirk formed on the bouncer's face. He wasn't looking at Frog; he was looking past him. Schemes was stuck in the grip of the other bouncer. He was trapped with his arms in the air in a full-nelson.

"Frog, behind you!" Schemes screamed, trying to warn him. It was too late. Before Frog could turn around, he was cracked in the head with a bottle. Fragments of glass flew everywhere from the bottle bursting from the impact. Frog thudded to the ground as the dude he was fighting stood over him with the neck of the bottle in his hand.

Maybe that would calm him down.

Ghost, oblivious to the rumble taking place back at the club, was with Shareef at his luxury estate. After meeting up back at the hotel, the two of them went to Shareef's house to talk business.

Ghost was taken aback by the astounding house. They pulled inside a black, lion-faced gate and went around a sputtering fountain when they parked the Maybach.

Inside, the house was immaculate. The fluffy carpet made Ghost feel like he was walking on clouds. The glistening chandelier and white walls made the crib feel like a white heaven as a cherry-almond aroma pervaded the air. The kitchen was like a marble and granite showroom.

They sat in the kitchen, eating a gourmet meal that had been prepared by Shareef's staff. The two of them enjoyed the five-star meal while indulging in a rather interesting conversation. By now, Ghost had already filled him in on how he and his team got at a dollar. Without giving too much detail, he had shared stories about robberies that he and the rest of them had committed.

Shareef listened intently and liked what he heard. He was already considering using Ghost his team to assist him with something he was putting together. It involved a lot more money than what they were used to, so Shareef wanted to be sure they were ready for the job. The take would take more than heart; it would take brains as well. There would have to be precision in this job. One mistake and someone could end up locked down for a long time. That was, if they made it out alive —the tricky part.

"I like what I've heard so far," Reef said flatly. "I've been putting something together for a while now, Ghost. It took a lot of work. It's real big, Ghost, real big."

"Yeah?" Ghost listened, waiting for him to tell him about the plan.

Instead, Shareef caught him off guard when he asked, "Why do y'all call him Schemes?"

"Huh?" Ghost didn't see that one coming. He gave him the rundown on how Schemes had received his name while he was in prison after Shareef repeated the question.

"I see," was all Shareef rendered as a response.

He didn't like Schemes. He didn't know why, but he got a bad vibe from him. For that reason, he didn't want Schemes to be a part of the job he was trying to execute.

"I like your crew, Ghost," he said, not yet disclosing his true feelings about Schemes. "This job takes skill, Ghost. I've put a lot of planning into this. A lot of homework. Most of which is already done, but I still need a solid crew to move when I say move."

"What is it?" Ghost's curiosity kicked in. He was tired of the riffraff. He wanted to get to the point.

Reef ignored the question. "I see the most y'all ever took was a few hundred thousand—which isn't bad for you guys," he said before taking a bite. "But this here involves millions." He let that sink in for a moment.

"What's the take?" Ghost repeated his question in an even tone.

Once again, Shareef ignored the question. "There will be armed guards everywhere, and they are always alert. Things must be precise, or it could get ugly. You may have to shoot your way out of there, paint the city red if things go sour." He paused. "Are you ready for that?"

Ghost nodded, but was growing impatient because he still didn't know what they were supposed to be hitting. "You still haven't told me what the target is, man."

Finally, Reef told him, "It's an armored truck."

"That shouldn't be too hard," Ghost said boldly "When and where?"

"Well, we'll get into the details when the time is right." "And when is that?" Ghost furrowed his brow.

There was a moment of silence before Shareef broke it. "Okay, the take is in Philly. I'm going to fly back with you guys. We'll take care of things from there. But remember, we still got a few people we have to put in the dirt."

Ghost nodded, but he wasn't concerned about them right now. They were talking money, and money came first.

"How much are we talking?"

Not expecting the figure Reef shot at him, Ghost's eyes shot open excitedly when he said, "Twelve million...at least."

CHAPTER 17

Reese's cousin Terry had been with Reese and Mar a lot lately. He had a go-hard mentality, and, once Reese told him he had some drama, he was with it.

However, Terry wasn't getting no money, so he was hurting along with his cousin and Mar. Reese and Mar had trouble making ends meet ever since they had been going through it with Ghost. They couldn't hustle in the hood because the cops were still investigating the murders, and niggas wanted them dead. So, they squashed the little misunderstanding they had about the botched kidnapping and agreed to put their heads together to get some money.

With C-Note dead, things were even worse. He had been their breadwinner. They had relied on him for his moneymaking craft. Luckily, after he got killed, they still had his equipment: the computer, printers, plates, and other little things he had used to duplicate tender notes.

They had been present a lot of times while C-Note put together batches of the funny money, so they knew the basics of how he did it. However, lacking firsthand knowledge made it a little complicated to do, but that didn't stop them from trying.

They didn't do a bad job for their first time. At least, they didn't think so. It wasn't C-Note's quality of counterfeit, but it was good enough. Now that the money was put together, they needed a way to get rid of it.

They came to the consensus that it would be best if they went at hustlers to get the money off. Instead of doing small things like purchasing clothes and other accessories, they decided to buy a large quantity of drugs from dealers and resell it to others.

Reese and Mar knew quite a few hustlers who had weight, so they picked their prey carefully. They decided a Dominican named José would be the sweetest candidate to burn first. José was an older Spanish hustler known for having coke like he grew it in his backyard. He had a bad reputation for being burnt. Rumors were that he was often taken advantage of, but did nothing in return.

Reese knew, from dealing with José on numerous occasions, that the soft Hispanic wouldn't even count the money before making the transaction.

They arranged a meeting with José. Reese put in an order for two bricks of powder. Without hesitation, José told him he could cover it whenever he was ready.

They met at the McDonald's parking lot on Broad and Diamond Streets. The spot was better known as Club McDonald's because of late night gathering on weekends by hustlers and chicks from all over the city. Many drug deals and bodies dropped at the same very location.

"It's been awhile, my friend? How have things been going for you?" José asked, starting small talk.

"Good, good. You got that?" Reese cut to the chase. He was a little nervous, and the unexpected guest didn't help.

"Yeah, yeah. I got you, papi." José nudged his man who pulled a plastic bag from between his legs and passed it to Reese.

José turned the dome light on inside the car. "Check it out, my man. Pure, the best fish in town."

"Man, I know what you're working wit, Pop! Turn that damn light off before you get us booked out here." Reese didn't want the light on once he passed them the money.

José turned the light out. Reese, then, handed the chubby passenger the bag of money. Reese's heart dropped when the man opened the bag to take a look at its contents. Reese held his hand on the door handle, ready to make a run for it if they detected the funny money.

The passenger fondled with the rubber-banded stacks of money. He quickly thumbed through the money to be certain it was, in fact, money. Indeed, it was. Just not all real money.

"It's all there," Reese quickly assured them.

The bag contained $70,000. They had put real bills on the tops and bottoms of each stack. After a satisfactory inspection, the men shook hands, and Reese slid out of the car before watching them pull off.

Reese strolled to the awaiting car where Mar and Terry were reclined. A sly grin was spread across his face. Now, all they had to do was sell the load and turn the drugs into paper. Reese wondered why they hadn't been doing this before because of how sweet it was.

"Pop the trunk, so I can put this shit up." Reese hopped in with them.

"Good thing I didn't have to use this," he said, patting his waist.

"Yeah, right, nigga," Mar said. "They probably would have took that shit from you just like that bitch did."

147

Back down in Miami, the night was young. The sky was clear, and the warm air was creating a laid-back atmosphere. Everybody was cooling out in the pool. Ghost and Kia were the only two missing. They'd already vanished back into the hotel.

Frog wasn't in the water either. He was poolside, stretched out in a beach chair. As always, he had a chick with him. She was massaging his shoulders while he laid back and stared at the sky. Around his head was an ace bandage. After receiving stitches for getting hit with the bottle, he had gauze and an ace bandage wrapped around his head with an ice pack resting on top. The woman with him was the one who he'd met the night before being smashed with a bottle.

His team laughed at him for the ass whooping he got. The sight of the turban-like bandage around his head was hilarious. Even he had to chuckle about the incident. He never got the chance to get the guy back because security threw his ass out the club like Uncle Phil used to throw Jazzy Jeff out the house on *The Fresh Prince of Bel-Air*.

The couples, Reem and Toya and Schemes and Rita, were in the pool, cuddled up. Kia didn't spill her guts about the girls messing with one another, and they had yet to disclose their secret affair. They both knew the cat would come out of the bag sooner or later. Toya wanted to tell Reem, but she didn't know how to, so she would let actions tell it all.

Schemes and Rita hadn't made it official yet, but they were feeling each other, and, without putting it into words, they were becoming a couple.

Toya broke the snuggling with Reem and floated over to Rita and Schemes. Reem had no clue why she'd broken the embrace or what she was up to, which was why his eyes grew to the size of golf balls when she started grinding on Rita's ass.

Schemes's ego was crushed because he thought Toya had wanted him the whole time, but, come to find out, she and Rita had something going on.

Rita turned around and poked her ass in Schemes's crotch as she embraced Toya, and the two of them explored the rest of each other's bodies while locking tongues.

Schemes and Reem's confusion turned into lustful stares. Their manhoods rose to the occasion as their girls demonstrated that they were beyond bi-curious.

Now, Schemes knew why Toya was always giving him funny stares. The kissing, fondling, and touching made it clear that the girls were into each other, so Toya had her eye on him because she was jealous that Rita was all over him. She was feeling him out.

Toya broke off from Rita and swam back over to Reem.

"Damn, baby! I didn't know you got down like that." Reem stared into her eyes without breaking the eye contact.

"It's a lot you don't know about me," Toya said and licked her lips.

"Oh, yeah?" Reem couldn't stop smiling. "You're full of surprises, huh?"

She whispered in his ear, and then took him by his hand, leading him out of the pool. Her body dazzled in the lights as the water dripped off her body. They strolled by Schemes and Rita, who were still in the pool, whispering and giggling. Reem wanted to try his hand and get it cracking with all of them. He nodded his head, telling Schemes to bring Rita and come on.

Frog had watched the entire thing go down, from the kissing to them walking past him to go up the stairs. He knew what time it was and wished he could go with them.

It was Schemes's turn to get his little cousin back.

"Holla at you tomorrow, player," he said with a smirk on his face as he passed Frog.

"Damn," Frog said, letting it slip out by accident. The woman he was with smacked him in the back of the head to let him know she'd heard him.

CHAPTER 18

What Reese had pulled off on Fat José was being whispered about all over the city. People talked about how José was sweet and had been burned once again. It was obvious that José was scared to put in work on Reese.

But that was exactly what had the people talking. He had a stake out on Reese's head, and word was traveling fast. Everybody wanted to get at him and collect the reward—a hundred grand.

José's pockets were as fat as his stomach, and a hundred grand was crumbs to the cake he had. So to put it on the head of yet another nigga who had played him was nothing to him. José's motto was "Why get my hands dirty when I can pay someone peanuts to kill for me?" Niggas in the city killed over parking spots, so he knew they'd jump on the hundred he'd put on Reese's head.

Unfortunately for Reese, word of the bounty had yet to reach him. He and his team were already lining up the next victim to burn with the counterfeits. They figured José would take the loss on the chin, but, if he didn't, they would kill him.

They made another batch of the replica money. It took them a few days to make a large enough quantity, but, this time, the money came out better than the last one. They were confident that they could get the money off.

Reese contacted another connect he'd dealt with in the past. It was another Spanish hustler from North Philly named Suave. Suave owned a few detail shops and mini-markets throughout the city. But he moved plenty of coke and dope.

Suave was shocked when he got a call from Reese. He couldn't believe Reese called him asking to buy two bricks. He'd already heard about what Reese had done to José and about the money on his head. At first, he started to tell Reese no, but two things came to mind: Reese would come straight to him, making it easy for him to rock him and get that money, and he felt disrespected because now Reese was trying to play him, too, and, for that, he had to pay.

Suave told Reese to meet him down on Seventh and Tioga Street at one of his stash houses. There, he would kill him and collect the bread from José. It would be the easiest hundred grand he'd ever made.

"This shit is sweet," Reese said, turning the music down in the car.

"Turn this shit back up!" Terry said. "That's my shit." Young Jeezy's, *Recession*, was playing.

"Yeah, I know this nigga is going to be lunching," Mar agreed. Mar had dealt with Suave a few times. Their relationship had been solid up until this point. They usually dealt straight, so this would catch Suave off guard.

"Call him to see where he's at," Mar told Reese.

They were in a car Terry had brought after turning the last bricks over. The Cadillac DTS cruised down Erie Avenue approaching Seventh Street.

Suave picked up after a few rings.

"Where you at?" Reese asked him.

"I'm on Seventh Street, where I told you to meet me."

"All right. I'm bending the corner now. Is that you standing on the corner?" Reese asked, referring to a few dudes who were out.

"Naw, park up. I'm coming out now."

Just like last time, they had laced the stacks with real bills on top and bottom of every stack and bonded them together with rubber bands.

A man appeared and stood on the stoop of a house up the street. Unless Suave had lost a hundred pounds and a few inches, it wasn't him outside the house. He wore a hoodie and was looking up and down the block like he was looking for someone. He didn't see them sitting in the car down the street.

"There he go right there," Terry said.

"Is that him?" Reese said, asking himself more than anyone else. He squinted his eyes, trying to make out the man in the dark. After saying "fuck it," he double-checked his burner before hopping out the car with Mar. Terry stayed put. "Come on. Let's see if that's him."

They strolled up the block, side by side. Reese carried the bag of money down by his side. The man gazed at them as they approached. They could tell now that it wasn't Suave. It was a mean-faced Spanish dude wearing a hoodie draped over his head. His almond-shaped eyes wore an evil glare, and he had what appeared to be craters in his face. His hand was buried inside his hoodie pockets, and he was fidgeting with something. No doubt it was a gun. His face was balled up, spelling trouble. *What the fuck is his problem?* Reese wondered.

He should have never spoken. His voice didn't match the tough guy image he was trying to portray.

"Suave said come in," he said in a soft, squeaky voice. He turned to go into the house, but frowned when he didn't find them following him inside. "Come the fuck on!" he snapped, sounding like an angry eight-year-old.

"Who the fuck you talking to? Where's Suave?" Reese wasn't feeling the dude's tone. Tactically, Reese and Mar knew, if they went inside the house, they would never make it back out alive. It was no question if they were inside, Suave would count the money, so they were trying to do the deal outside.

"What?"

"Tell Suave to come to the door real quick," Mar said. He remained as calm as possible. The Spanish dude probably didn't pick up on it, but Mar and Reese could see the nervousness written on each other's faces and body language.

Tough Guy probably did pick up on it because he smirked and said, "Hold on," before disappearing behind the door which looked like it had seen better days.

"Yo! Let's get the fuck outta here," Mar whispered to Reese as soon as the dude went inside. Though it was frigid outside, beads of sweat sat on Mar's nose. "This shit ain't gonna work."

Reese nodded, but, as soon as they turned to leave, the door opened. Suave appeared in the doorway with this dumb-ass smirk on his face. Tough Guy was behind him, but he was too tough to smile. He was grilling them.

Suave frowned and asked, "What's the problem?"

"We didn't know who the dude was," Reese responded, referring to Tough Guy.

They all were standing on the curb now. The door was still open. Reese stole a glimpse inside. There were several more men sitting at a dusty-ass table. They looked as tense as the rest of them standing outside.

"Well, come on in." Suave nodded toward the door as he turned to return inside the house.

Suave and his men planned to get them inside and end things quickly. They weren't expecting Reese to have company, but, for a hundred grand, he could die, too. It didn't matter to them.

"Y...y...you got the work?" Reese stuttered out. He could have smacked himself for being so nervous.

"Of course, I do. Don't be silly," Suave said confidently. "Now, come on in. It's biting out here."

Reese didn't know what to do, and Mar's silence and blank facial expression showed he didn't have a clue about what to do either. They both knew one thing, though—they couldn't go inside the house.

As if by miracle, Reese's phone went off.

"Yo!"

He picked it up with a sigh of relief. He gave Suave and Tough Guy his back while he talked on the phone. Terry was on the other end of the line.

The others didn't know who was on the phone, but Suave showed his impatience. A hundred grand was standing right in front of him.

Mar watched as they looked at Reese like a piece of bread. He wasn't feeling the vibe he was getting from them, but then, he didn't know if it was that or his own nervousness. The tension grew thicker by the second. Mar knew Reese was buying time, but he, also, knew it was about to run out.

As if Suave's patience wore thin, he walked up the steps and told Tough Guy, "Handle that."

Tough Guy nodded. Reese ignored them, keeping his back turned to the three of them. Terry had seen them turning around, so he called Reese's phone to see what was up.

Mar's eyes shifted to and from Tough Guy to Reese. Tough Guy's hand came out of his pocket, and a black handgun was clutched in it. He raised it to the back of Reese's head and squeezed the trigger.

"Reese!" Mar screamed in sync with the explosion of the gun. At the same time, Mar smacked Tough Guy's hand down. A split second later, and Reese's life would have been a wrap. Reese spun around to find them wrestling over the gun. A car engine revved to life and tires screeched from down the block.

Reese pulled his gun from his waist and tried to shoot Tough Guy, but he couldn't get a good shot because he was wrestling with Reese. He started shooting at the windows and doors of the house Suave was in. He knew that they would be on their way out, so he fired before they could.

The gun the two were tussling for went off a few more times. Mar banged Tough Guy's hand against the hood of a parked car until he broke his grip, and he dropped the gun. The weapon skidded out into the middle of the street.

Terry was just as amped as the others; he pulled the car up, but flew by them a couple houses before stopping. He threw the car in reverse and backed up so fast that he flew back past where they were a couple of houses before stopping.

Reese and Mar broke out into a sprint into the street and jumped inside the car.

Reese dived in the backseat. Mar slid across the hood of the car and jumped in the passenger seat. Terry slammed on the gas, and the car's tires hollered before the car took off.

Terry forgot to put the car back in drive and was caught off guard by the car reversing instead of going forward. He lost control of the wheel and slammed into a parked car. After gaining his composure, he threw the car in drive and peeled off. Just as he was doing so, Suave and a load of his men emerged from the doorway, skipping the steps. They were shooting at the car as it tried to escape.

All Reese, Mar, and Terry could do was duck and say silent prayers that they didn't get hit by the bullets bursting out the windows and piercing the side of the car. They dropped the guns when the car crashed, so they were defenseless.

Tough Guy was crotched in the middle of the street, picking up his gun when the car raced dead at him. His screams were no match for the car's grill as it smacked him. Headlights were the last thing he saw.

A crunching sound was made, and the car lifted up as they finished Tough Guy off. That didn't make Terry let up on the gas. They whipped wildly off the block and disappeared into the night.

Reese felt a burning sensation in his leg. His entire pants leg was covered with blood when he looked down.

"Yo! I'm hit!"

Mar looked down, feeling all over his body to see if he was hit. "Me, too!" he said. "I think." His shirt was covered in blood,but he couldn't find where he was hit.

"Me, too, Terry whispered faintly before losing consciousness.

He car lost control, swerving and gaining a breakout of angry horns. Mar grabbed the wheel from the passenger seat as they sideswiped several cars.

"Get his foot off the gas!" Reese panicked.

They tried to bring the car to a stop. A light pole took care of that as they smashed into it. Everything went white. For a second, they thought they were dead, but, luckily, it was the airbags coming out.

They scattered out of the car.

"Help me get Terry," Reese said.

"He's dead, man. Let's go!"

Reese checked his pulse and found that it was beating lightly. "No, he's not! Help me!"

They wanted to get Terry out the car, but sirens were getting closer and closer.

"Come on. We have to go!" Mar yelled.

Reluctantly, Reese left him, and they ran from the scene. The plan was a disaster.

And now they had another enemy.

CHAPTER 19

"Boy, don't come busting in here like that!" Lindell snapped. "And why the fuck have y'all got all that blood on y'all?"

Reese's mom was on the couch high as a satellite when they came rushing in. She had a rundown three-bedroom brownstone on Devon Street. Although Lindell was a crack head, she was well-respected in the hood. Devon Street was right off of Locust Avenue where she ran a speakeasy, selling liquor and all types of prescription drugs. This was where Ghost used to cop his drug of choice before his beef with Reese.

The blood Mar and her son were covered in didn't worry her one bit. They were moving, so as far as she was concerned, they could carry their asses right back where they came from. Lindell had the nerve to be fussing about someone busting in her house unannounced when her door stayed open, inviting the whole hood in.

Reese and Mar ignored her and ran downstairs to the basement. They were forced to leave Terry at the scene because the law was coming. They hoped he was still alive. They ended up stealing a car from a gas station to get home.

They stripped out of their bloody clothes. Reese kept seething and wincing at the pain as he took his jeans off. Once they were both out their clothes, they broke out laughing. Reese's wound was no more than a flesh wound; it was only a graze. Mar checked himself, and, to his surprise, he hadn't been hit at all. The blood on his shirt had to have come from Tough Guy. He must have gotten hit when the gun went off while they were wrestling for it.

They had to laugh about the entire situation. But, when they thought about Terry, things weren't funny any more.

Everybody was back in Philly after balling out of control down in Miami. After the trip, they were even more determined to get more money. Shareef took the flight back with them.

It was time to get down to business. However, Schemes wasn't included in the job, and it was bothering him. Ghost and Reem were off somewhere with Shareef, and Schemes couldn't believe he wasn't invited to the meeting. He was taking that personally. Although he didn't know Shareef too well, he felt like his boys should have told him about whatever they were up to.

Frog and Feeq were pressing him about doing a bank robbery, but, for more than one reason, he declined. They were family, but, instead of going outside the circle, he had stayed loyal. Feeq wanted him to do a job with a CO, and he wasn't with that.

Schemes was even more hurt by the fact that he had held Ghost down while he was in jail, and, in return, Ghost turned his back on him to mess with Shareef. Reem didn't do anything for Ghost while he was gone, but look who Ghost had by his side. *Unbelievable*, Schemes thought.

"Shit! I'm the one who put all of this shit together." Schemes patted his chest, talking to himself. He'd been pacing back and forth for several minutes in his living room. "And this is how they do me!"

He snatched his phone from the table and dialed out. "Frog, where you at?"

"In the crib. Damn! What's up? What time is it? Why you calling me so early?" His voice crackled.

"Stop bitching, nigga!" Schemes told him. "I'll be there in twenty minutes."

"What? You better not!"

Before Frog could object, the line went dead. Schemes was already out the door.

Shareef didn't waste time running the plan down to everyone. Though things were more complicated than the other robberies, the crew was still with it. Initially, they were skeptical because things seemed too good to be true. However, they knew that, at any second, things could go wrong and turn into a blood bath. Still, with the money involved, the risk was outweighed by the reward. Shareef was the mastermind of the job. Though he wouldn't be getting his hands dirty, he was responsible for putting everything together.

The day was just right for the job. The clouds captured the sun, and the temperature was perfect. Still, beads of sweat escaped Ghost's pores, resting on his forehead. The mask he wore hid the nervous expression on his face. He couldn't help but wonder if the others were as nervous as him.

The armored truck they were robbing was cruising at a normal pace. It traveled the usual route. The truck's guards were locked and loaded with itchy fingers waiting for someone to try them. Armored trucks and banks were robbed on a daily basis in Philly, so the guards and police were always alert.

Ghost and the team were on point. They couldn't show any signs of nervousness or hesitation because, if so, the robbery could turn into a segment of the movie *Heat*.

Reem was fidgeting with the Mossberg shotgun. He didn't look like his usual self. He had the face of another man. The bulge under his shirt showed he had a vest on.

The other guy, Trev, who was one of Shareef's men, was in the front, driving. He was driving like he didn't have a care in the world. Over objections, Shareef had sent him on the job with them, but they had really wanted Schemes to go with them. They didn't want to break up the crew, but Shareef insisted on Trev's involvement. They knew Schemes was hot about them leaving him out, but they intended to break him off.

The truck turned off Spring Garden Street onto Columbus Boulevard. It was pulling up to the spot where it would make its next drop. This was where it was going down. "It's time to get this paper," Ghost said.

"Fresh outta the Federal Reserve," Reem added with a nod. The truck slowed before coming to a stop. "Here we go," Ghost said, looking at Reem. The two of them jumped out with the Mossberg pump shotguns.

Frog was laying in the bed, half-asleep. He couldn't get back to sleep after Schemes woke him up. He knew something was wrong because of the early morning call and because his cousin was on his way to his spot so early. He'd, also, heard the urgency in Schemes's voice and instantly knew something was up.

The TV had been on all night. Frog knew *The Price is Right* was on although he was under the covers. He heard the Showcase Showdown wheel spinning. The door damn near flew open when someone started banging on it like they were the police.

Frog got up and opened the door for Schemes.

"Damn, nigga! You banging on the door like the po-po." Schemes ignored him and barged inside. He was flaming. He plopped down on the bed in Frog's room and went right into things. Frog had half of a Dutch of weed in the ashtray, and he lit it up.

"Who told you to light my shit?" Frog barked.

"Nigga, you're in here laying around in your damn boxers, watching *The Price is Right*," Schemes said, but double looked at the screen to check out one of the show's models.

Schemes took a drag of the weed before saying, "Man, these niggas are about to come up on something nice, but they won't tell me what. They cut me out." He let the smoke ease out of his mouth and nose.

"What are you talking about?" Frog was puzzled. He slipped some jeans and a T-shirt on.

"Ghost and Reem are up to something with Shareef, and they didn't put me on."

"How you know?"

"They fucking told me. Yeah, these niggas told me they didn't need me. But they kept bragging about how big it was."

"Yeah?" Frog was shocked because they always moved together. "What you think it is?"

"I don't know, but I'm gonna find out."

"Cool out. You know they're going to break us off, so calm down," Frog said.

"That's not the point. I put these niggas on taking money, so how they gonna move without me?"

"Cuz, you act like you need them to move with or something. I've been tryna get you to put me on for a minute now, but you be brushing me off." Frog knew this was his chance to convince his cousin to do a sting with him.

"That's exactly why I came over. I'm gonna put something together, but first we gotta go see Feeq."

"Why we gotta see him?" It wasn't that Frog didn't want to see his peoples, but he didn't know what seeing him had to do with taking some money.

"I'll explain it on the way up there. Get yourself together, so we can roll."

Schemes was hesitant to tell him that he was going to see Feeq to set things up with Smitty. He didn't want to do a robbery with him, but they needed a third man. He knew Smitty wanted to move because Feeq was bugging him about it, so it was either find someone else or put Smitty on the team. Frog would definitely have something to say, so he was trying to think of a way to tell him.

The Price is Right went off, and the twelve o'clock news came on afterward. Schemes was reclined on the bed and Frog was getting ready when the news caught their attention.

"Hi, this is Amy Taylor, reporting live from CBS3 Eyewitness News. I'm here live at an abandoned warehouse on Columbus Boulevard. As you can see here in the background, police and FBI agents are on the scene, investigating what they are calling an armored truck heist.

"Moments ago, a Lumbar armored truck was discovered in the warehouse behind me. Apparently, an armed guard, who was on duty driving the truck, has been found bound with handcuffs inside the truck. According to police, the guard was uninjured and will be taken to FBI headquarters for questioning.

"From what we have been told so far, the truck was found after being tracked by a GPS tracking device equipped inside the truck. The truck was idle for over thirty minutes, and police were contacted to investigate the unusual incident.

"A substantial amount has come up missing from the truck. The amount has yet to be determined, but police are saying the loss is expected to be in the millions.

"Authorities are in search of two armed guards who are employed by Lumbar Services. Those two men, Darmacus Stoves and Charles Wright, have not yet been labeled suspects, but they are persons of interest and expected of foul play.

"If you have any information regarding the whereabouts of these individuals or facts surrounding this robbery, the police are asking you to contact them by dialing the 1-800 number on your screen. As details unfold on this matter, we will keep you updated. For more information visit our website at CBS3.com, thank you. I'm Amy Taylor, reporting live form CBS3 Eyewitness News. Mary, back to you."

Schemes and Frog sat there, staring at the television in shock. They couldn't believe their eyes or ears. They looked at one another in silence for a second.

"You think it was them?" Frog asked.

"It ain't no fucking coincidence."

CHAPTER 20

Hours earlier...

The warehouse smelled like a basement. The air was dank and polluted with a mildew aroma. The walls were brown, covered in dust, giving them a rusty look. A rusted staircase went up to a balcony, which looked like it would collapse at any second. The windows were covered with a dull-green coat of chipped paint and equipment scattered about.

Shareef, Reem, Ghost, and Trev sat at a table, discussing the plan to take down the armored truck. Spread across the table was a blueprint of the Federal Reserve Bank located in Center City. Next to it was a map displaying the route of one particular truck.

Surprisingly, Trev was the one who was running the show. He pointed out things on the map to let the others know where everything was located inside the bank. Trev had been employed by Lumbar Services for the last four years. He and Shareef were good friends. They had agreed to take down one of the trucks before recruiting the others.

A bulletin board was in front of the table with rows of pictures pinned to it. The pictures were of the truck, of the location they would rob, and, most importantly, of the two guards, Damarcus Stoves and Charles Wright.

The two guards were new to the truck service. There were pictures of them, their families, cars, houses, and a picture of every angle of their faces and bodies. They seemed to be oblivious to the fact that someone was taking pics of them. According to Shareef, he'd captured these shots during what he called fieldwork. The plan was to frame the two guards. They were going to make it appear that the guards were crooked and had pulled off the heist of the truck. In order to make that work, they had to get rid of the guards for good.

That morning, the guards were kidnapped and murdered, and their bodies were disposed. This way, when they tied Trev up in the truck, the cops would believe him when he told them that the other two guards with him had committed the robbery. They're families would be questioned, but, just as planned, they would say their husbands left for work normally and never returned. It would appear as if they took the money and left the country. In reality, they would be dead and gone.

As they stood to execute the plan, Ghost spoke up again, saying, "I still think we should bring Schemes in on this." Reem nodded his head in agreement. Shareef had expressed his lack of trust in Schemes and didn't want him involved in the plan.

He snapped, emphasizing it again. "We don't need him. I don't like or trust him." He patted his chest for emphasis. "I followed these niggas to put this together. I'm the man!"

Ghost and Reem were dressed just like Trevor. They wore matching armored guard uniforms. Their chests were bulging with the vests they wore. Name tags were pinned to their shirts with the guards' first initials and last names.

The most clever part of the robbery were the prosthetic masks Ghost and Reem wore. They were cloned to look exactly like the two guards. They looked so real that a person would think they were actually the real people they were molded to look like. The masks were like the ones worn by Tom Cruise in *Mission Impossible* and Angelina Jolie in *Salt*.

Shareef was behind getting the masks created as well. He was a master of the take. Ghost and Reem's complexions matched those of the guards as well.

There was another person involved, a guard named Richard, who was the one who released the money after getting the signatures of the guards leaving the Reserve. He would let them sign out and take the money as if he saw nothing suspicious, making the job even more possible to pull off.

"All right, remember what we went over," Shareef told them. "You guys must make every stop normally before we reach the point where we move. The truck will be on a GPS, so, once you get to the warehouse, we must move quickly to empty the truck and get out there before the law shows up."

Everyone understood and was ready to go.

"All right. Let's get this paper," Shareef said.

Inside the underground floor of the Federal Reserve, the three men strolled down the corridor. They were headed to the garage where the trucks were loaded. The corridor reminded them of a prison cellblock because everything was steel and cement.

Occasionally, they got a glance at the loads of money in the rooms as they passed by them. Trev was used to walking through the bank, so he remained calm, but Ghost and Reem were nervous as hell.

They passed a room that looked like it had a three-layer sheet of Plexiglas on it. Inside, they could see the stacks of money being loaded in bags. It looked like too much money to count. Ghost looked at Reem, and, for a second, he thought he was the guard Demarcus. The mask looked that real.

The Reserve had state-of-the-art security equipment; cameras were mounted overhead throughout the entire building. Instinctively, they kept their heads down as much as possible to avoid them.

The plan seemed to be converging just as planned. They had the guards' keycards, which they had taken before murdering them. However, they let Trev do most of the opening of doors.

They were approaching the garage door up ahead. It was almost over; they'd made it through the bank as stealthily as possible. As they made their way down the last hallway, they heard footsteps behind them. Chatter from walkie talkies erupted as well. At the same time, they passed a security guard posted on the wall. The short, stocky officer was clad in the same uniform as them.

"Good morning," the officer greeted as they passed. Trev spoke back while Ghost and Reem simply nodded.

Reem was a bit nervous and removed his hand from his pocket. They turned in unison to see what the commotion behind them was. For a second, they thought that they'd been made and that it was about to go down.

Luckily, they were relieved when they saw a few technicians run into one of the rooms behind them.

"We have a glitch on machine 26B," one of them yelled before disappearing into the room.

Ghost let out a sigh of relief, but, as soon as they were about to go in the garage, the stocky guard yelled, "Hey!"

Ghost looked at Reem. Both had the same look in their eyes. Reem gripped the Mossberg tighter and was getting ready to go postal.

Trev looked at him and lightly shook his head.

They turned to face the guard.

"You dropped something," he said, nodding toward something on the ground.

They all looked at a keycard on the ground. It must have fallen out of Reem's pocket when he pulled his hand out of it. Reem was so nervous that he hadn't even noticed that he'd dropped it.

He bent over to pick the card up.

"Thanks," he told the officer.

"New, huh?" the guard asked, picking up on his nervousness.

"Yeah," Reem answered flatly.

"I can tell. Loosen up a little; it's not that bad."

Reem gave him a nod before the three of them disappeared behind the door. Once in the garage, they signed the truck out and left the back without incident. Richard let the gate rise and saluted them from the booth as they pulled out into Center City traffic.

Once back at the warehouse, they had to move quickly. While they were gone, Shareef cleaned the warehouse up, getting rid of the maps, bulletins board, etc.

They were greeted by Reef as they entered the warehouse. He stood on the balcony over the top of them, giving a round of applause.

"Good job, gentlemen," he said, shaking his head.

Quickly, he joined them, and they started uploading the money from the armored truck into a van with DAISY'S FLOWERS scrawled across the side. While the three formed a line to pass the money down, Shareef hopped inside the truck's rear compartment. He used plastic and tape to plant the fingerprints of the two armed guards they were framing all around the inside of the truck.

"Let's move, gentlemen!" Shareef shouted. He looked at his watch after jumping out the truck. He knew they were on the clock before headquarters would realize something was wrong with the idled truck. He had a digital trunking scanner equipped with J-Band capability, so he could hear if a dispatch went out over the airwaves to police.

"Let's go! Let's go! Let's go!" Shareef yelled, rushing the others.

They handcuffed Trev and secured him in the back of the truck. His feet were, also, bound with zip-ties. All he had to do was play his part when the police showed up.

The rest of them hopped in the van and were gone. They pulled out on Columbus Boulevard as multimillionaires.

CHAPTER 21

The following day, Reef and Ghost relaxed at a property Shareef owned in Philly. It was a small redbrick home that looked like it would collapse at any minute, joining the others on the block. However, stuffed in a back room was enough money to buy the whole block.

"Tomorrow, I'll fly back down to see my man," Shareef said. "He'll turn the money over for us." Reef was referring to a money launderer down in Miami. Because the money was fresh out the Federal Reserve Bank, they had to launder the money, so it wouldn't be traced back to them.

"We got a little over fifteen million. With his cut off the dollar, we should end up with about two-point-five a piece," Shareef said.

Ghost heard what Shareef was saying, but he was in his own world. He nodded his head, but he was stuck in deep thought. He still couldn't believe he was a millionaire. It felt like he was a millionaire. It felt like he went to sleep and woke up rich. But, last night, he didn't get any rest because the thought of having all that money wouldn't let him.

"Snap outta it, baby boy," Shareef told him. "So, what you plan on doing with all this money? You can't fuck it up. You have to do something with it, invest in something. You don't want to blow the paper and have to do something else. That would be foolish."

"So, why did you decide to do this robbery after all you have?" Ghost asked inquisitively.

Reef thought about that for a second before answering.

"You know what? You have a point. Taking money is repulsive, Ghost. I have done well for myself over the years, but, for some reason, I love the take." He sat there in silence, thinking about how his youngin' had just pulled him up. Just when he thought he knew it all, Ghost had given him something to think about. He tried to tell himself he was done with the game, but he knew it was highly unlikely. He loved taking money, and he had graduated to the level that he didn't have to get his hands dirty. He could simply put the plan together and get others to put the work in. He thought about how far he'd come, from doing petty stick-ups with Ghost's father to the truck job they'd just finished. The thought made him think about Ghost's dad.

"So have you heard anything from your pop?" He knew Ghost didn't feel his pop like that, but he asked anyway.

"I think I may invest in some real estate," Ghost said, trying to ignore the inquiry about his dad.

"That's good. But what's up with your dad?" Shareef persisted.

"I don't know, and I really don't give a fuck." "What?" Shareef asked, frowning his face.

"Come on, Reef. You know how I feel about that." "I know. I know, but I know he loves you, so—"

Ghost cut in aggressively. "He don't love me! He loves the streets! He loves smokin' that shit!"

Reef butted back in, and Ghost's nostrils flared up, demonstrating his anger. Reef raised his hands for Ghost's silence.

"Listen, Ghost. You're what? Twenty-five, twenty-six, right? You were born in the eighties, baby boy. That was the crack era. I know you've heard a lot about those days, but you have no idea what it was like back then. Me and Khalil," he said, referring to his pop, "did a lot of dirt together." He paused as if he was recalling some of those moments. "I remember when he met your mom. I remember when you were born, man."

Ghost plopped down on the couch, listening to his old head. "When crack hit, Ghost," Shareef paused and looked straight into Ghost's eyes, "there were only two sides of the fence to fall on. Unfortunately, your pop made the worst decision of his life. He experimented one time. The drug had the streets going crazy, and he tried it once and never bounced back. I hate the decision your dad made as much as you, but he's my man, and I owe it to him to be there for him. You do, too, Ghost. I know firsthand how much he loves you, so don't kick that shit about how he doesn't love you 'cause it's not true. He lost the same game we're playing. A game that loves no one."

Ghost understood what his old head was saying, and he thought about it for a second. He was swaying between love and hate for his dad, but he knew Shareef was right, so he agreed to go see his father with him.

"All right. Listen. I'm going to fly south to take care of this paper. Everything is set up for you and wifey out in the mountains, so go have a good time. By the time you get back, I'll have this paper cleaned up. Then, we can go see your pop. And don't forget we have to take care of that situation," Shareef said, talking about getting at Reese and Mar. "For now, go lay low, and we'll take care of that when we get back together."

Ghost agreed, and the two of them embraced before departing. Shareef had a membership to a North Lake Tahoe private community home. He was letting Ghost take Kia out there on a short getaway. They needed the time alone, and Ghost was anxious to go.

But not killing Reese and Mar was the worst thing they could have done.

The Beneficial Bank was aligned amongst a row of other stores and establishments inside the plaza. Schemes, Frog, and Smitty were slouched in the black Buick Century behind its dark tinted windows. People scurried to and from the stores.

Schemes had put together another master plan. Though reluctant to move with Smitty, the extra body was needed. Smitty would play a minimum role by staying in the car and having it ready when they were coming out the bank. Frog wasn't feeling Smitty's involvement, but he decided to go with Schemes's plan.

"This is gonna be like taking candy from a baby," Schemes said as they watched the bank closely.

"So, when do you wanna move?" Frog asked. He was ready to go.

"We can take it down on the first rainy day." "What we gotta wait till it rain for?" Smitty asked.

"Because it will be easier for us to get in without anyone paying attention. Plus, with the cameras in the parking lot, we'll use umbrellas to block us from them, and no one will see us with our masks on before we go in."

"Damn! You're a genius," Smitty stroked his ego.

Schemes loved the adulation. "That's why they call me Schemes, baby," he said, feeling himself. "So, we have to watch the weather to see when it's going to rain."

Schemes started the car and pulled out of the parking lot. His phone started ringing, and he answered it.

"Yeah," he answered flatly after seeing it was Reem calling.

"What's good, nigga?" Reem was excited.

"Ain't shit. What's up?" Schemes didn't hide his lack of enthusiasm.

"We on, nigga. That's what's up!"

"I ain't on, nigga. Y'all on!" Schemes retorted.

"Come on. You know we got you. Stop acting like that. We tried to talk to Shareef, but he said we didn't need you." Reem didn't want to tell him that Shareef didn't trust him and that that was the reason they didn't let him do the truck job with them.

"But we got something nice. Ghost told you, right?"

"Naw, I haven't heard from him since the other day."

"Oh, he's on vacation," Reem told him. "Vacation? We just came back," Schemes said.

"I know, but he's with wifey. They went out to Cali or something. Shareef got a condo or something out there."

Jealousy and envy ran through Schemes's veins. He knew they had come up on something nice, and Ghost didn't even call him yet. Schemes would never admit it, but he was acting like a bitch.

"So what's up with you, though?" Reem asked.

Schemes couldn't get out of his feelings, so he answered, "Ain't shit. I'm trying to eat like y'all."

"I can dig it. The money is being cleaned up. I got you after it gets washed up, so sit tight, homie."

"All right. That's what's up. I'll holla at you later." They hung up, and Schemes looked at Frog, shaking his head. Frog didn't know who was on the phone with Schemes, but he figured it was either Ghost or Reem because he could tell his cousin wasn't feeling them by the conversation.

"Who was that?" Frog asked.

"Reem," Schemes answered. "This nigga talking about sit tight and he got me. He got me fucked up."

Schemes was jealous as shit. He knew they were going to break bread, but that wasn't the point. They had left him out of the biggest job yet, and his pride wouldn't let him accept that. He had put them on to taking money. Now, since Shareef came along, they had left him hanging. As far as he was concerned, Reef could go back into the hole he came out of.

"So, we still gonna get this money, right?" Frog asked.

"It ain't no question. They don't call me Schemes for nothing," he said. He turned the music back up and turned to Rick Ross' "Stay Schemin."

"Staaayyy Scheeemin," he sang along with the hook.

CHAPTER 22

Though warm outside, the wind whirled outside the old-fashioned cabin. Ghost and Kia were sunk in a plush leather couch, cuddled and watching the fifty-two inch plasma television mounted over a double door fireplace.

"Did you have fun, baby?" Ghost asked her.

"Yeah, when I was on my feet," Kia joked.

The two of them had just come from skating in an arena inside the private community.

They caught a private jet courtesy of NetJets to the hills out in Cali. The jet was delightful, but was superseded by the astounding cabin resort. The stay in the mountains was so serene. Kia's jaw dropped in her chest at their arrival.

"Well, I hope you are not too sore tomorrow because we're set to go hiking in the mountains and mountain-bike riding." Kia looked at him with an unsure look on her face. She couldn't even remember the last time she'd ridden a bike, and she'd never been hiking, so it would be quite an experience.

Times like this made Kia love Ghost, but she hated the life he was living. She had already lost Kha's father to the streets.

She thought about the possibility of losing Ghost, and she knew she would never be able to bear another loss like that. Besides Bird, Kha looked up to Ghost, and she wanted him to be a good role model. Bird kept Kha while they were away again. She didn't know Ghost was a millionaire now, and since he was planning to leave the game alone for good, her worrying was in vain.

Kia started kissing on Ghost's neck and rubbing his abdomen. He invited her affection by lifting his arms to allow her to peel his shirt off. Blood rushed from his thighs, giving him an erection. His manhood stood at its peak, forming a tent in his Polo boxers. Kia showed him her love as she kissed his chest. Slowly, she lowered herself to his abs before sliding his boxers down.

Standing full length, his piece ran the length of her entire face as she licked his balls. His scrotum rushed together at the attention of her warm tongue. She seductively ran her tongue up the shaft of his penis and wiggled it on the tip while looking up into his eyes. She jerked him for a second. She knew her teasing was driving him insane.

Finally, she took him into her mouth and went to work. He ran his fingers through her hair and guided her head as she went along. She jerked him with one hand at the same time.

She removed her hand and deep throated him as far as she could. Not satisfied with the inch or two unattended to, she came back up and bobbled her head back down until he completely disappeared in her mouth. Spit dripped down his balls, and she blew on it to create a tingling sensation.

"I love you, babe," escaped Ghost's lips. "Oh, baby, I'm about to nut." He held the back of her head, guiding it, but she did most of the work. Kia loved the power of making her man squirm and moan. He finally let loose, and she didn't miss a drip.

He stood up, looming over top of her. Taking her by the hand, he guided her from her knees and planted his face where her thighs met. She straddled her legs over his shoulders while he pleased her.

"Oh, yeah! Right there, baby," she cried. Her wish was his command. Juices streamed down his chin, but he ignored them. He took her swollen lump in his mouth and sucked her just the way she liked. He slid a finger inside her and found her g-spot. She flinched at his touch.

"Oh, my god! Oh, my god!" She sounded like a broken record as she incessantly called out in vain. "I'm cumming, baby." And she did.

"Please, baby," she begged him to travel inside her.

"Tell me you want it," he said, teasing her.

"I want it! I need it!" she whined some more.

Finally, he entered her, and her wetness swallowed him whole. Pushing her legs as far back as her pliable joints would allow, he ran in and out of her.

"Oh, my god, baby! You're going to make this pussy explode!" If that was possible, he was definitely on the verge of causing an explosion. As she had a series of orgasms, her eyes rolled into the confines of head.

He turned her around and punished her from behind. The movie was going off, and the music played during the credits. Kia threw her ass back to the beat as she enjoyed the mixture of pain and pleasure.

"I'm about to cum," Ghost squealed.

"Cum in me. I want to have your baby," Kia revealed. Ghost let everything loose, and he collapsed on her back as she laid on her stomach. They breathed heavily, trying to catch their breaths. Ghost had been waiting for the right moment to propose to her, and, as they laid there as one, he popped the question in a light whisper, saying, "Marry me."

The words were like music to her ears. She'd been waiting forever for this moment. A single tear escaped her eyelid. The answer didn't need to be said.

Schemes laid in the backseat, listening to raindrops tap against the roof of the stolen minivan. Frog slouched in the rear compartment with him. The two of them wore black ski masks as they hid behind the tinted windows. Smitty sat in the front seat, tapping the steering wheel. He was nervous as can be.

"You ready, Frog?" Schemes asked.

"Yeah, let's do it," Frog responded eagerly. They hopped out the van and put their umbrellas up to stay undetected more than block the rain. Schemes gave Smitty his chirp phone before getting out the van; they could chirp him from Frog's phone when they were ready for him to pull the van to the bank's front door.

Schemes's eyes scurried across the parking lot.

"I told you. Look. No one is paying us any attention," he told Frog, who looked around quickly before putting his head back down before anyone saw him wearing the ski mask.

Schemes opened the door of the Beneficial Savings Bank and brought the umbrella down in front of his face as he entered the bank's vestibule. Inside, the employees were conducting business as usual, oblivious to the entrance of the robbers. By the time they looked up, it was too late. Guns were out, and the men were moving at breakneck speed.

"Everyone get the fuck down!" Schemes demanded. He pointed the gun at an employee who seemed to be in shock. She still hadn't gotten down on the ground. "Get on the fucking ground!" he repeated.

This time, she obeyed.

The rest of employees and customers were already buried in the carpet. None of them looked past the weapons in their faces. The tellers were secured behind security glass a few inches thick. They didn't get a chance to react before Schemes had a blonde chick that was working the open floor by her hair at the Plexiglas security door.

"Open the door," he said calmly. The tellers behind the door hesitated. Obviously, they were safe, so they were considering whether they should open the door or not.

Schemes became frustrated and pushed the blonde's head up against the glass door. He put the gun to her head, and, holding it to her temple, he repeated, "Open the fucking door!"

One of the tellers looked into the blonde's eyes, and, without words, he could see her silent pleas for them to comply. All the blood drained from her face as she became ashen. She seemed relieved when she heard the door being unlocked. Schemes shoved her around once inside the tellers' station. Then, he smacked the male teller, who opened the door, in the head with the gun, sending him crashing to the floor with the blonde woman.

"Open the fucking drawers, now!" Schemes took a folded laundry bag from his waist and stuffed the money in it after the tellers opened the drawers.

"Are there dye packs in this money?" he asked, but the money was already in the bag anyway.

"No," a teller cried.

Schemes glanced at Frog, who was standing by the front door. Frog had his back against the wall, so no one could see him from outside.

"Where's the manager?" Schemes asked.

An older female got up from the ground.

"Open the vault," he told her.

"I can't. It's on a timer. It can't open until ten o' clock," the manager said.

Grabbing the woman by her collar, he told her, "Don't fuck-ing play with me!" He slammed her into the metal vault door and demanded, "Open the fucking vault!" Tears trickled down the woman's face.

"Please! I swear! I can't! Just take what you have and go!" the lady cried.

Schemes looked at his watch. It was 9:43 a.m. There was no way that they could stay inside the bank for twenty minutes. "Fuck!" he shouted, causing the victims to flinch.

He shoved the manager, and she tripped over another em-ployee who was face down on the ground. She hit the floor hard and buried her head in her palms. Schemes ran from behind the glass and nodded at Frog, who pulled out the phone and chirped Smitty.

"Pull up. We're ready."

Schemes was sick. He couldn't believe he'd fucked up. He knew the money from the tellers' drawers wasn't shit, especially not split three ways.

They watched the van pull up, and they exited the bank, hopping into the stolen getaway vehicle. As instructed, Smitty pulled off regularly to avoid tracking unwanted attention.

Frog and Smitty sat in the front, smiling ear to ear and cele-brating the take. However, Schemes knew that the job was a fuck up and that they'd only gotten away with pennies.

A popping sound erupted, and they all looked around to find out where the sound came from. A sizzling sound seethed and suddenly a reddish smoke permeated the van's interior. Schemes looked down and found the smoke coming from the bag of money. As if things weren't already bad, they'd gotten worse. Schemes had made the mistake of grabbing a dye pack when he was grabbing the money.

The billowing smoke transformed the entire interior of the van to crimson-red. The smoke burned their eyes like they had been sprayed with pepper spray. They could barely open their eyes from the overwhelming burning sensation. The smoke hindered their breathing as well.

"Throw it out! Throw it out!" Smitty begged. He could barely see the road, so he wanted Schemes to throw the bag out. He didn't care about the money. He couldn't stand the burning and confusion the dye pack smoke was causing. The van swerved recklessly on the rainy tarmac. Angry horns blared, and cars weaved to avoid the wild vehicle.

"Throw it out!" Frog shouted along with Smitty.

"No! Drive, nigga!" Schemes demanded, refusing to throw the damaged bag of money.

Instead, he balled the bag up in his arms like a running back carrying a football, closed his eyes, and tucked his face and the bag in his lap and shouted, "Drive, nigga! Drive!"

CHAPTER 23

Schemes, Smitty, and Frog finally reached the switch point without getting arrested. Staying low-key was out of the question. Once Smitty rolled down the windows to let the smoke out, the van looked like a red ball of smoke, flying down the street. As if Mother Nature sensed chaos, the rain starting coming down even harder.

The van skidded to a stop on a small block, and the three of them jumped out the van as if it was getting ready to blow up. Smitty heard a clicking sound as he jumped out the driver's seat. He looked down in time to see the Boost Mobile phone hit the ground, along with the umbrella that had been resting in his lap. The phone slid under a parked car, adjacent to the getaway van.

He picked the umbrella up before looking under the car to get the phone. However, the phone was out of his reach. Sirens could be heard not far away. Without a doubt, the police had a description of the stolen van, so they needed to get out of dodge before they were spotted.

"Come on, nigga!" Schemes yelled in frustration from the Buick Century that he and Frog were already sitting in. They saw Smitty reaching under the car, but didn't have a clue what he was doing.

"Fuck the phone," Smitty said and jumped to his feet, leaving it behind.

After diving in the backseat, he slammed the door, and they fled the scene. All of them had traces of red dye on their clothing and skin. Schemes's beard had traces of the dye, making it look like he had red henna in it.

"Yo! What the fuck was you doing under the car?" Schemes asked, keeping his eyes on the road.

"I dropped the phone when I got out the car."

"You what?" Schemes couldn't believe his ears.

"Man, that shit was on my lap, and it slid under the car when I hopped out. I was tryna get it, but I couldn't reach it, so I said fuck it," Smitty responded.

The phone was subscribed to Schemes's name, so he was infuriated by what Smitty was telling him. First, the safe. Second, the dye pack. And lastly, the phone had been left at the scene. If found by the authorities, the phone would definitely be a solid lead for them.

Schemes's conscience was killing him. His intuition had told him over and over not to do a robbery outside the crew. But they had left him hanging, and his pride wouldn't allow him to accept that, so he had recruited Frog and Smitty. Now, he was paying for it.

Now, he knew he had to lay low because the feds would be coming.

Ghost and Kia stood in the window of the cabin, enjoying the panoramic view of the mountains. The cabin was stationed at the top of the mountains, so they could see the cabins, trees, and roadways below. Ghost felt like he was on top of the world.

He held Kia in his arms as he gazed over her shoulder out the window. Life had been going great for him over the last few months. He had everything he wanted. The thought of leaving the game alone played heavily on his mind lately.

"It's beautiful, isn't it?" Kia asked.

"Not as beautiful as my baby," he said, planting a kiss on her neck.

She smiled from the compliment. "Wish we could live like this forever."

"We can," Ghost assured her.

She chuckled and responded, "We can't live off Shareef forever."

Ghost was a bit appalled by her response, but he still hadn't told her he was a millionaire. "We don't have to, baby. I told you I would always make sure you and Kha were all right."

"I know, Ghost, but I want you here with us. None of this means anything if you're not here with us."

"Baby, I'm done," he told her. "We are set for the rest of our lives. I will never leave your side again."

"You promise?" Kia asked, as she looked down at the five-carat ring on her finger. She had waited her whole life for the day she got married, and that day would be coming soon.

Ghost promised her that he would never leave her again and that he was done with the game. Little did he know, the game loved no one, and trouble was waiting for him back at home.

Terry laid in the hospital bed, irritated by the sounds of the machines. He had an IV in his arm, and his side was killing him. He had been hit three times and was lucky to still be alive. Despite his injuries, he would have left the hospital on his own if it wasn't for the handcuffs holding his arms to the bed's side rail. A uniformed officer guarded his room to prevent his escape. He knew he was in a jam because he'd been charged with the homicide of Tough Guy.

Two plain-clothes detectives walked in the room.

"How are you, son?" one of them asked. Terry just nodded. "As you know, things aren't looking too good for you." The officer let that sink in before continuing. "Now, you can help yourself out here if you give us your side of the story." After taking Terry's silence as reluctance to cooperate, he said, "We know there were others with you the other night. Obviously, this was a case of self-defense because you were shot at the scene, but your partners left you for dead. Help us identify them, so we can ask them a few questions."

"So, if I let you know what you want to know, you're going to help me?" Terry asked.

"Uh-huh."

Terry paused as if he was considering the option. "I only know their nicknames," he told them.

"Okay, that's a start," one of the detectives said, pulling his pen and pad out. "Okay, go ahead."

"Hairy," Terry told him.

"H-a-r-r-y?" he asked.

"No, H-a-i-r-y." Terry spelled it out for clarification. Then, he gave a brief description of him.

"All right. Who's the other one?"

"Balls," Terry said, telling on his other accomplice and giving another physical description.

In return for his cooperation, the detectives turned the hospital television on for him before leaving to go find the two others involved.

These two dick heads really left looking for Hairy Balls?

CHAPTER 24

The rain started to dry up from the late morning sun. A sea of red and blue lights were at the scene of the bank robbery. FBI agents Vito Boselli and John Graham were among the authorities investigating at the scene. Actually, the two agents were at the scene where the stolen getaway van was discovered. There weren't many clues back at the bank, so they left to investigate the van.

The agents knew bank robberies were a repetitive crime, so it was likely that the suspects behind this job were responsible for others previously done or would commit more in the future. Still, they needed a break that would lead them to the suspects.

"This one looks like some amateurs, Vito," John told his partner, looking at the candy-red-coated insides of the stolen van.

"What's the report on the van?" Vito asked.

"Still not reported stolen. But the ignition is damaged, so we're pretty sure it's hot. They probably got it late last night, so the owner may not even realize it's gone yet. The plates are registered to a John Lee."

189

"Sounds like an Asian name. Has anyone tried to contact Mr. Lee yet?"

"Yeah, but no luck reaching him," John grimaced.

"The victims back at the bank said the men were using phones which sounded like walkie-talkies," Vito said.

"Sounds like they had Nextel phones."

"Fuck! We're at another fucking standstill!" Vito snapped. He was a very moody agent. One second, he was calm, and then, out of nowhere, he was flipping out. He was renowned at FBI Headquarters for his fifteen years on the job. Specializing in robberies and kidnappings, he was the best in the field. However, robberies typically yielded little to no evidence. Most robbers wore masks and gloves, making it almost impossible to identify them.

"Let's get the van down to headquarters to get it dusted for prints and vacuumed for hair samples. We'll probably come up empty, but do it anyway," Vito instructed another agent on the scene.

"We need a break," John said.

"They'll make a mistake. Trust me. They always do."

Vito was a cocky asshole. He knew the robbers would fuck up and, when they did, he'd be right there, waiting to bust them. Just as John nodded in agreement, they heard a phone ringing, but didn't recognize the ringtone as any of theirs.

Once they realized the ringing wasn't coming from either of their phones, they looked around in confusion. The ringing was close by, so they immediately started searching the van again. They'd already combed the van, but didn't find a phone, but they searched again.

The ringing stopped, but they didn't stop looking.

"I'm not fucking crazy! I heard something ringing," John said, frustrated that he couldn't find it.

"I heard it, too."

Just as they were about to give up, the phone came back to life. John desperately ripped the van apart. Vito dropped to his knees and looked under the van.

Nothing.

About to climb to his feet, Vito turned his head to look under the parked car next to the stolen van. The bottom of the car was lighting up from the phone's light. Vito dropped to his belly, not caring about his cheap suit and grabbed the phone.

He got his pudgy ass up and stared at John. He wasn't sure if he should answer it. John nodded, giving his approval for him to answer the phone before it stopped ringing. Vito shrugged and answered, "Hello."

"Damn! This nigga ain't answering his phone," Reem said to himself. "Baby, have you spoken to Rita today?" he asked Toya, who was in the car with him.

"I spoke to her a little earlier."

"Was Schemes with her?"

"I don't think so. I didn't ask, but I doubt it 'cause she was on her way to get her hair done when I talked to her."

Reem had called Schemes's phone several times throughout the morning, but wasn't getting an answer. He'd had a premonition. For some reason, he knew something was wrong. It wasn't like Schemes not to answer the phone.

Reem even tried Frog's phone, but got the answering machine right away. He tried Schemes's phone one last time. To his surprise, he finally got an answer.

"Hello."

"Yo! Who is this?" Reem didn't recognize the voice on the other end.

"This is Special Agent Vito Boselli." Vito let his title sink in before continuing, "Reem, we have your partner down here at the FBI headquarters." He lied. "He fucked up big time, and, from the looks of things, he's not biting the bullet." Vito knew the person calling was Reem because it popped up on the screen when he called. He, also, knew Reem couldn't know he was lying about having his man in custody because if he knew his man had lost his phone, he wouldn't even be calling it.

Vito knew Reem was silent because, besides breath, there was silence on the other end of the phone.

"Why don't you come on down and have a little chat with us?" Vito tried his hand.

Still silence.

"Are you there?"

"Eat a dick!" Reem asserted before hanging on him.

Schemes, Frog, and Smitty made it back safely to Smitty's spot. They agreed to go there after the robbery because it was closest to the bank they took down.

Frog and Smitty broke their phones to pieces because Smitty had dropped Schemes's phone at the scene. Although Smitty didn't have a chirp phone, he had used his phone to call Schemes, so he had to get rid of his phone, too. They knew the feds would check the calls and locations of the phones that were in contact with the recovered phone. It would be easy for the feds to get the phone company to give them the cell tower information to pinpoint the location of any phones that were in contact with the phone Smitty had dropped.

"How the fuck did you drop the phone, dick head?" Schemes snapped.

"It was on my lap, man. When I got out, it fell. That fucking smoke and rain had me discombobulated. I tried to get it, but I couldn't reach it."

Schemes just shook his head. He still couldn't believe Smitty had dropped his phone. He knew the feds would find it at the scene and come for him. It was time for him to get low.

They took the money out the bag and saw that it was ruined. The majority of the money was covered with the red dye. They tried several tricks trying to get the dye off the money but to no avail. They counted it anyway. It only totaled a small nine grand. Even worse, only a good two grand wasn't destroyed by the red dye.

"We gotta burn this shit," Schemes said.

"What? We ain't burning no paper!" Frog retorted.

Smitty agreed, but he was in a shell, so he didn't say shit. He was upset with himself. Here it was he finally got put down, and he had messed up big time.

"We can use the money for something," Frog insisted. Schemes just huffed and puffed. Honestly, he didn't want to

get rid of the money either. However, the decision to get rid of the money was a bit easier for him because he had more than both Frog and Smitty put together. Greed kicked in, and he had done the worse robbery yet.

"Come on, y'all. Let's get outta here," Schemes said.

"Where are we going?" Frog asked, knowing they had to get low before the feds came.

"Anywhere but here," Schemes told him. He shot Smitty an angry glare and shook his head again. "Smitty, where are you going to go?"

"Shit, I don't know." The nervousness could be seen all over his face. "Where y'all gonna go?" Smitty asked.

Schemes shrugged his shoulders. He really didn't know where he was going to go yet either. But he knew it was far away from there.

"Grab what you're going to grab. You can roll with us," Frog told Smitty.

Smitty nodded before disappearing to get his things together to leave.

"What are we going to do?" Frog, then, asked his cousin.

"I will come up with something," Schemes assured him.

"Go get the car ready. We'll be right down," he added.

Frog stood to leave as Schemes went upstairs where Smitty was.

"Come on, Smitty. We're out," Schemes yelled as he climbed the steps.

Frog was just on the other side of the door when he heard a single gunshot. He paused, about to go back inside. But his intuition told him to go start the car. He already knew what had taken place. Schemes had blown Smitty's head off.

CHAPTER 25

Schemes and Frog were riding down the street in silence for a few minutes before Schemes finally said something about killing Smitty.

"I had to do it, cuz."

Frog just nodded. He didn't care too much about Smitty being dead, but he was worried about still being broke. It had been awhile since he'd hustled, and the few grand he had was running low.

"I know I'm going to have to hear Feeq's mouth," Schemes continued. "I didn't want to fuck with that cop-ass nigga anyway. I had to do it, cuz. He would have told."

Frog nodded again. "Fuck that nigga!" he said. "Now what?" "I don't know. We gotta put something together, though,"

Schemes told him. "First things first. I gotta go grab a lawyer 'cause them boys are gonna be on my heels."

The thought of that gained a sigh from Frog. "Listen, cuz. I'm fucked up. I know you got paper still. We can't do shit with the money we just got, so you may have to give me something to lean on until we get right."

"I got you."

"Should we tell Ghost and them?" Frog asked, looking at him with his brows raised.

"I was thinking the same shit. We have to. We can't leave them in the dark about this shit. They might be hot now, too," Schemes said. "I wanna say *fuck 'em*, but I gotta tell them."

"We still gotta get some paper, though."

Schemes ignored Frog's statement and said, "We gotta stop to grab some new phones."

Frog persisted, "Man, what we gonna do. I can't live off you." "I'll put something together," Schemes said, squinting his eyes and shaking his head.

The stolen minivan crept down the same street for the third consecutive time. Still, the bystanders and early-goers paid the van no attention as it disappeared and reappeared several times.

Schemes sat behind the wheel of an inconspicuous Chrysler Town and Country minivan. Glued to the passenger seat, Frog peered out the window, clutching a handgun inside the pocket of his hooded sweatshirt. They both watched consumers enter and exit the Wells Fargo bank. They stared at the bank like hunters leering at game in the woods.

Because they wanted to be cautious, this was the third time they had circled the block to watch the financial institution and its surroundings. They were moments away from making their move to take the bank. The van was drowned in silence as the two of them focused on the task a hand. The only sound inside was the chatter coming from the police scanner they had for police detection.

"What are we waiting for?" Frog asked. He was anxious and ready to go, but was following his cousin's lead.

After the botched robbery a few days ago, they decided to take another crack at it. Without the third body as a getaway driver this time, things would be a little more complicated, but they were sure they could pull the sting off. With Reem and Ghost being self-made millionaires and claiming retirement, they only had one another and more innocent victims were about to be victimized.

"Chill, we're going to spin the block one more time and then we're going in," Schemes responded. He was being more meticulous this time. The last time things went terribly wrong: dye packs, the lost phone, and Smitty ending up in the morgue. He was attempting to avoid any of those mishaps on this job. They had the FBI in pursuit, so one slip up could lead to being housed at the Federal Detention Center in downtown Philadelphia.

As they passed the bank the fourth time, they were stopped by a red traffic light. Traffic began to get heavier as the time dug deeper into the morning. A gold Buick Sedan came to a halt next to them at the light. Though the windows of the sedan were tinted, two male figures wearing baseball caps could be made out inside. The men inside the Buick glanced at them in the van several times, but were trying to hide the nosey looks.

Schemes instantly grew suspicious. "What the fuck are they looking at?"

Frog took a look and kept his eyes locked on the sedan and now the men matched his stare. The light seemed as if it would never change.

"Man, who the fuck are these dudes? I swear this is the second or third time I seen them." Frog eased his gun out of his pocket. Schemes was already nervous because they were about to rob the bank, but now the stand-off was adding to things. He put his hand on Frog's.

"Relax," he told him. He knew Frog wouldn't hesitate to open up on them, but he didn't want to lose focus and spoil what they came to do.

The tension eased up once the light turned green and the cars pulled off. The sedan switched lanes, getting behind the van. Schemes peered through the rearview mirror at the car behind him, but dismissed his paranoia when they made a right turn and the car didn't follow.

"We're good. They kept going," he told Frog.

"I was getting ready to let loose on them," Frog said. His weakness was moving without second-guessing. He considered it going hard, but, one day, his go-hard philosophy would bite him where the sun don't shine.

They spun the block one more time.

"All right. You ready?" Schemes asked.

Frog nodded. They eased up the block and got ready to pull into the bank's parking lot when chatter erupted on the digital trunk scanner. A call shot across the airwaves with a description of the van, including its license plates. The two men in the sedan were undercover police officers, and they became suspicious of the van after seeing it circle the bank several times. The Chrysler was described as a suspicious vehicle with two male occupants in the vicinity of the Roosevelt Mall.

"That's us!" Frog said, his eyes popping out his head.

"No shit, Sherlock!"

They broke out into sheer panic. They had been detected and had no clue how. They had guns and all kinds of accoutrements for a robbery in their possession, so a confrontation with police was the last thing they wanted. Shooting it out was before prison on the option list.

They turned down a side street to escape the busy avenue and, as soon as they did, they saw the gold sedan again, this time, coming out of the plaza. Immediately, they put two and two together and knew the men in the car were undercover cops. They had called them in and requested back up in the vicinity.

Schemes eased his Timberland boot down on the accelerator, and the car flew down the small block. He whipped the car into a parking spot, and the two of them emerged from the car as if it was about to explode. Just as they were walking up the street, the gold sedan turned the corner nearly on two wheels. Schemes and Frog stopped dead in their tracks.

Trying to remain calm, they pulled their guns out and held them down by their sides out of sight. It was about to turn into a heated scene.

They refused to go to jail. The streets would turn into a warzone before they allowed that to happen. Surprisingly, the sedan regained its composure and rode right by them. They figured the cops didn't know they were made and wanted to wait for backup to arrive before they revealed their identities. Little did they know, thanks to the police scanner, they were already made, and Schemes and Frog were a step ahead of them.

Sirens could be heard approaching. The heat was on. The Buick stopped at the corner before slowly turning. Schemes and Frog knew they would be back. But when they did, it would be too late.

The suspicious men would be gone.

Terry was sick. Not literally, but he couldn't believe he was down for a body. He was jammed up this time. The police had found him at the scene in the car that he ran Tough Guy over with.

Luckily, he wasn't charged with first-degree murder. He was fortunate enough to be facing third-degree murder charges. The district attorney's office wanted him to cooperate with them to find his accomplices, but he wouldn't budge.

He was in the hole for cursing out one of the correctional officers. He'd only been down a weekend, and, already, he was on lockdown.

His cell was popped open for his hour of recreation. A few other inmates were out for their recreation as well, but he didn't know any of them, so he didn't kick it with them. He showered and went back to his cell.

Meanwhile, Rico and Shiz were out for their hour of rec, too. They both got ninety days in the hole for the rumble they got in. Time flew in the bucket. They spent hours passing time by reading books, playing cards, and talking shit. They had managed to get in the same cell in the hole, so that was love.

Although they didn't know Feeq too well, they knew him. They all were from uptown, too. Feeq had been holding them down since they were in the twist. He sent them countless books, something to smoke on, and commissary since they were on commissary restriction. They knew he didn't have to do that, but, ever since Rico had seen him in the hallway, he had been showing love. They grew love for Feeq, so, when he sent a few novels down the other day with a note in it asking for a favor, they were on it.

The short letter was stuck inside Rahiem Brooks's, *Die Later*. Feeq wanted them to put some work in on someone named Terry. According to Feeq, Terry was in the hole with them. They didn't know who he was, but it didn't take long for them to find out. It was the quiet one who'd been in the hole for a week or so. They didn't know what the beef was over, but it didn't matter. No questions asked, it was time to move.

Rico was down for attempted murder. He'd stabbed a guy eighteen times with a kitchen knife. Luckily, the dude had lived, so it was still light at the end of the tunnel for him. He lived by the sword, and the one he was strapped with right now was about to be put to work.

Shiz, on the other hand, was down for a body. He was trigger-happy and pulled it on anyone for anything. He didn't have a shank at the time, but Rico did, so he was moving with him. He picked up a floor brush as they made their way to Terry's cell. They'd just watched him get out the shower and go inside his cell. With the element of surprise on their side, a shank, a floor brush, and Terry's dumb ass in shower shoes, Terry didn't stand a chance.

Terry was standing in the mirror, putting grease in his hair, when he saw the two men approach his cell door. From the looks on their faces, he knew they weren't coming to say what's up. Besides, the banger and floor brush in their hands gave them away.

The one with the knife approached first. Terry got off one clean punch, catching the dude square in the jaw before they could attack him.

That made Rico madder. They beat him relentlessly.

Ghost was back from Cali. Life couldn't be sweeter. Shareef had gotten the money cleaned up while he was away, so he was officially a millionaire.

He and Reem were riding in his brand new Audi A8. He brought two—one for himself and one for Kia—when they came back. Kia had settled for the smaller A4.

"I'm done, Reem. It's over for me, man. We up now. You should leave the game alone, too, dawg," Ghost advised his man.

"I know, dawg, but this is all I know. I mean, think about it. What are we gonna do now? It ain't like we can just up and leave the game alone," Reem retorted.

"Why not?"

Reem was at a loss for words. He didn't know why he couldn't leave the game alone. He hadn't even given the option much thought until now.

"You got a good girl, Reem," Ghost said, referring to Toya. "We're rich, dawg. Who would have ever thought we would have been here? It's time to be smart about things." "You're right. So what are you gonna do?"

"I'm not sure, but I know it's a wrap for me. I'm getting married. That's enough for me to fall back right there, dawg. Me and wifey have been talking about buying into some franchises or something. You should do that with us. We can pull Schemes and Frog in, too, and then we can all leave this shit alone," Ghost said.

"Man, Schemes is hot right now," Reem said.

Schemes had told them about the fuck up he had made. All except the part about Smitty's involvement.

Schemes knew they would never forgive him for riding with Smitty.

Not only was he from outside the circle, he was a CO. He didn't want to tell them he rode with a cop and that he had to blow his head off. Smitty had made the crucial mistake of dropping the phone, but Schemes lied and told them he dropped it. He only told them that he and Frog had participated in the job.

Schemes didn't know whether Smitty's body had been discovered yet, but he was laying low anyway. He had hired a lawyer. The lawyer told him the feds would be looking for him, if not to arrest him, at least for questioning. Either way, Schemes didn't want any parts of that, so he and Frog were laying low. Besides Reem and Ghost, they didn't call anyone else. Schemes didn't even bother to call Rita. Not even Ghost and Reem knew of their whereabouts.

"I know Schemes fucked up, but that's still our boy, so we have to look out for him," Ghost asserted. Loyalty was everything to him, and he refused to turn his back on his childhood friend. "When this shit blows over, we can put him on something legit," he continued.

Reem knew he was right, so he nodded in agreement. "So what kind of franchises are you talking about investing in?" he inquired.

"I'm not sure yet, but I was thinking about some Subways and Rita's Water Ices," Ghost told him.

"That sounds good. Just let me know."

Ghost nodded and pulled his phone out his pocket to answer it. The caller ID said it was a blocked number.

"Yo!" he answered.

"Nigga, you thought this shit was a game?" the unknown man on the other end said.

"What? Who the fuck is this?" Ghost asked.

"Watch your mouth, nigga. I got your bitch, nigga!" the man said.

"What?" Ghost asked, not sure if he had heard him right. The man on the other end sounded like he was disguising his voice.

"You heard me! I got this stinking-ass bitch here, and, if you don't do as I tell you, I'm gonna blow her fucking head off! You'll never get any of this sweet pussy again!"

"Who the fuck is this? Stop playing wit me, nigga!" Ghost still didn't believe what he was being told. He thought someone was playing a prank on him. But talking about kidnapping his fiancée wouldn't be humorous.

"Nigga, you think this is a joke?" The unknown man's voice sounded like he had a cold or his nose was stopped up or something. Ghost tried to make out his voice but couldn't.

"Baby! Help me! Please!" Kia's voice erupted into the receiver. "All right. Shut up, bitch!" the man said, snatching the phone back from her head.

"Who is this, Reese?"

"You guessed it. The devil in the flesh."

Ghost instantly got dizzy. He couldn't even think straight. Reem stared at him. He knew something wasn't right. Ghost pulled the car over because he couldn't even drive anymore.

"If you hurt her, I will kill you!" Ghost contended. "Shut up, pussy! I'm running the show. Now, listen—" "Reese, I swear to fucking god. If you touch—"

"What did I say?" Reese shouted into the phone. "I will kill this bitch right now. Say something else, nigga."

"All right. All right. Don't hurt her, man," Ghost pled. "What do you want? Anything! I'll give you anything you want, Reese. Just don't hurt her."

"Stop bitching, nigga!" he told him with a wicked giggle.

Ghost knew the person responsible for this had to be Reese. He was the only person who would want to do something like this to him. He silently vowed to stop at nothing to avenge the kidnapping of his fiancée.

Ghost took a deep breath before asking again, "What do you want?"

"I want a quarter million. I want it by tomorrow, or you can say goodbye to this bitch for good." He sounded serious. "I'll call you back with the time and location."

"All right. Just don't hurt her, man," Ghost begged.

He was talking to thin air. The line went dead.

CHAPTER 26

"They got her, man," Ghost said and turned to Reem.

Reem knew what it was. He was so angry that he couldn't even say anything. Just like Ghost, he was silently blaming himself. He knew he should have pressed more to kill Reese and Mar. Not getting at them sooner had come back to bite them in the ass. First, they had tried to kidnap Toya, and now they had grabbed Kia.

"So, what are they talking about, man?" Reem asked, concerned.

"This nigga talking about he want a quarter million."

"When and where?"

"He didn't say. He said he would call me tomorrow with the place and time."

"I'll put half of the money up, man," Reem told him.

Ghost just nodded. He knew Reem was just showing his loyalty because they both knew the money wasn't an issue. The quarter million was peanuts. The safety of Kia was more of a concern. They both knew Reese and Mar were dangerous, so it was no telling what they would do.

Ghost thought back to the conversation he'd had with Shareef. He had told him the only rule to war was to win, and Reese and the crew were showing they were trying to come out on top. The ransom demand was the only good sign. At least, it didn't appear that Reese was going to kill Kia because he called with a ransom. If he wanted her dead, she would be gone already. Ghost hoped he was right. Of course, the possibility of them killing her after getting the money remained.

"We gotta tell Reef and Schemes," Reem said. "We're going to get her back," he added, patting Ghost's shoulder.

"After that, you know what we gotta do."

Ghost nodded. What was understood didn't need to be said.

Kia was knocked out cold for hours. She wasn't sure how long she was asleep because the basement she was in was nearly pitch black. The windows were sealed and covered, blocking the sunlight out. Besides, she had a blindfold covering her eyes, and her mouth was gagged. Her legs were numb from being in the same position all night. Both her arms and legs were tied to the arms and legs of a chair. It took her forever to get to sleep, and she was surprised she did. The basement was dank, giving the air a moist feeling. The sound of water dripping every few seconds eased her to sleep.

Finally, she was awaken by the sound of a creaking door. Footsteps followed, and, by the sound, she could tell it was more than one person.

"Well, good morning, pretty lady," one of the men said.

Kia was frightened by their presence. She was shaking compulsively and couldn't bring it to a stop if she wanted to. She nearly jumped out her skin when one of them touched her. *Toughen up, bitch. Kevin is going to get you outta this*, she told herself.

"Relax, I'm just taking off your gag," one of them told her. She tried to remain calm, but she couldn't stop shaking. She felt nauseous and started sweating profusely.

"Please, just let me go," she cried once the gag was removed. "In due time, pretty lady," one of them said. She couldn't see them because she had the blindfold on, but she could tell only one of them was talking. It sounded like the guy was disguising his voice. It sounded as if the kidnapper had a mouthful of tissue or something to change his voice.

"Here. Chew on this," the kidnapper said, putting a granola bar in her mouth.

Kia was reluctant to eat whatever it was she was being given because she couldn't see it and didn't know what it was she was being fed. However, the sound of the wrapper crumbling let her know it was food, and the sweet taste on her tongue once he shoved it in her mouth was undeniable. She gobbled the whole bar down as he fed it to her. Then, he gave her some water. He couldn't lift the bottle to her mouth as fast as she was guzzling the water. Her mouth was dry, and her lips were chapped from going hours with nothing to drink, so the water was a blessing.

"Damn, girl," he joked. "All right. Put her gag back on," he said to his accomplice.

Before he could get the towel tied back around her mouth, she started vomiting all over herself. She gagged like her entire insides were being thrown up. Instantly, she felt better, like the weight of the world had been lifted off her shoulders.

"What the fuck! Are you all right?"

Kia shook her head before pleading with the men holding her captive.

"Please, let me go," she cried in a whisper.

"Sorry, this isn't about you. It's about the money and that no-good nigga of yours. This will be over today, depending on how your man plays."

Kia snapped, yelling, "Motherfucker, Ghost is going to kill you! I swear on everything I love—you're going to rot in hell!"

That earned her a smack across the face, leaving blood in her mouth. She spat it on him, which gained her a closed fist the second time.

"Put the gag back on this bitch!"

The other man did as he was told.

"Let's go make the call before I kill this bitch!"

The two men left the basement and almost instantly Kia started crying. She began feeling nauseous again and started perspiring.

What the hell is wrong with me? she wondered.

Not only was she being held captive, but little Ghost growing inside her was, too.

Special Agent Vito Boselli was sitting at his desk going through a file about a series of robberies committed in the Philadelphia area. He was the best at what he did, and he was determined to solve the string of robberies.

"Vito, we got those records back from the phone company for that phone we recovered at the Beneficial Bank job," Special Agent John Graham said, entering Vito's office.

"What about the DNA and hair samples?" Vito asked without raising his head from the file.

"Nothing." John hated to tell him.

"Do we have a profile put together on this Hawkins guy?" Vito finally looked up, showing some interest.

"Yeah. He lives in the Northwest Division, or, at least, that's the address we have listed for him."

"Looks like we have to pay someone a visit," Vito declared, getting up and snatching his suit jacket from the back of the chair.

"Do you wanna put together a task force?"

"Naw, not yet. We'll pay this guy a visit, ask him a few questions, and obtain a DNA warrant to see if we can come up with a match," Vito said.

"Yeah, let's go. We got our man now," John said before they left the office to find Schemes.

Bird was watching Khashan once again. However, he'd left him with his mother, Khashan's grandmother, for the time being. Right now, he was with Ghost and Reem back at Ghost's place.

Ghost, Reem, and Bird practically sat in silence while awaiting the phone call from Kia's abductors. They already had the money for the ransom counted and in a duffle bag.

"Have you heard back from Frog or Schemes yet?" Reem asked, breaking the silence.

"Naw, not yet. They wanted to come as soon as I told them, but they're hot, so I told them to lay low. They're going to fuck around and get us all jammed up. We don't need that kind of heat right now," Ghost answered.

"What about Shareef?"

"He's supposed to be flying in today. He offered to pay the ransom himself, but I couldn't let him do that. I told him we had it covered."

Ghost's cell phone started ringing. The three of them looked at each other, and then the phone. Bird nodded at Ghost to get it. Bird was just as anxious to get his sister back and retaliate against the men responsible for her disappearance.

Ghost looked at the phone's screen.

"It's not them; it's Schemes," he said, disappointed.

"Yo!" he answered.

"What's going on? Is everything all right? I mean have you heard anything from Reese and them yet?" Schemes asked, concerned.

"Naw, they haven't called yet. This shit is driving me crazy, man."

"Listen, Ghost. I know I fucked up big time. I was on some nut shit, but, if you need me, I'm here, man. Them niggas gotta pay, dawg," Schemes said sincerely.

"I know, I know. Don't worry about that now. Where are you? As a matter of fact, don't even tell me. Just lay low, man. This shit will blow over. How's your money looking?"

Ghost had nothing but loyalty to his team. He knew Schemes and Frog were laying low and couldn't do much. Because of that, he knew they couldn't move how they wanted to in order to make ends meet, so he was willing to make sure they were good. Schemes told him that he was still good financially.

"What about Frog?" he asked.

"He's good. I got him," Schemes replied. "Hold on. He wants to speak to you."

"What's up, big homie?" Frog greeted Ghost.

"Man, this is driving me crazy," Ghost responded.

Ghost was a living example that money didn't bring happiness. Here he was a millionaire, but it seemed like, just as he reached new heights, his world had come crashing down. Money didn't mean anything without Kia.

"I feel you, man." Frog sympathized with him. "I know what you're going through. We will make them niggas pay for this, man," he added."Listen, I got some paper for you, Frog," Ghost told him. "I know things are tight for you, and I don't want you to do anything else crazy, so I'm going to give you something to hold you down."

Frog didn't reply right away, so Ghost asked him if he'd heard him. "Yeah, I heard you, man. It's just...it's just here you are going through a crisis, and you're still tryna make sure I'm good," Frog said.

As they were talking, the other line beeped on Ghost's phone. He read the screen and saw a blocked number.

"This may be them. I have to take this call." Ghost clicked over before Frog could even respond.

"Yes," he answered.

"All right. Listen closely," Reese said. "Do you have the money?"

"Yeah."

"Of course, you do," he said, snickering.

"I wanna speak to my wife," Ghost informed him.

"Shut up, nigga! I'm running the show. You'll talk to this nasty bitch when I say so, pussy," he retorted with a lot of animosity.

Ghost bit his tongue. He wanted to flip out on him, but, because he was in no position to do so, he played along.

"Okay, I got your money, man. Please let's just get this over with," he pleaded. "And don't hurt her, man."

"Stop bitching, nigga." Reese seemed to be taunting him rather than trying to get the exchange over with.

Sensing Ghost's impatience, Reese said, "All right. Here's the deal. You and only you, take the money to the abandoned Taskykake Factory down on Hunting Park. I know you're not dumb enough to call the cops, but leave those trigger-happy boys of yours at home."

"All right. I'll be alone, but I want to speak to her."

"What did I tell you?" Reese snapped, sounding like he had a mouthful of food. "I'll let you talk to her when I'm ready.

Now, no guns, no company, and no cops! Eight o'clock. Tastykake Factory. Alone!"

Then, the line went dead. Again.

CHAPTER 27

The sun was just past setting. Ghost had a plethora of emotions going on inside him. He was nervous, angry, and frustrated. The emotions were written all over him. He felt guilty for getting Kia involved in this. He had to get her back.

He looked at the clock on the radio, which read 7:53. He'd shown up early to the abandoned warehouse. Anxiously awaiting the phone call, Ghost constantly kept looking down at his phone. The ten minutes he had been waiting seemed like forever.

Finally, the phone rang, and he nearly jumped out of his own skin from the sound of its ringer. It was dark. He was strapless, alone, and worried half to death about his fiancée's safety. *Relax.* He took a deep breath.

"Yeah," he answered calmly.

"Are you in place?"

"Come on, man. What do you think? Let's get this over with." Ghost was tired of the games and small talk. "I got your money. Now, let me speak to my wife to make sure she's okay."

Ghost could hear the phone being fumbled with before Kia's voice came into the receiver. "Kevin, please get me outta this," she begged. She sounded weak and tired.

Ghost's eyes flooded with tears, but he stayed strong. "I will, baby. I promise. This is almost over. Stay strong," he told his fiancée. The phone was snatched away from her before she could respond.

"All right. Listen. Drive to the back of the warehouse. There, you will see a dumpster. I want you to put the bag of money in it and leave. Don't come back. If you do, she's dead," he instructed.

"Hold up! Where is she? Let's do the exchange at the same time. How do I know you won't kill her once I pay you?" Ghost asked.

"You don't," he answered sharply. "Relax. If I wanted to hurt this bitch, she'd be dead. This has nothing to do with her. This is between you and me. Now, do as I said. Put the money in the dumpster. As long as the money is right, we're good. The next call will be from your bitch."

"But—"

Ghost banged on the steering wheel in frustration when Reese hung up on him once again. He let out a sigh before grabbing the bag of money and getting out the car.

Special Agents Boselli and Graham had had no luck finding Schemes for questioning. They checked the address on record for him, but came up short. However, they were able to speak to his grandmother, who told them that Schemes hadn't resided at the address for several years now. Besides that, she refused to answer any further questions and claimed that she had no clue about the whereabouts of her grandson. She insisted her baby wasn't into any criminal activity whatsoever, but the agents didn't believe that for one second.

Surprisingly, though, the agents received a call from an attorney asking questions and informing the agents he was representing Donald Hawkins, the man they were looking for. Apparently, the card they'd left the suspect's grandmother with their contact information on it had made its way into the hands of an attorney. That definitely confirmed their man-of-interest's involvement.

"Let's cross reference this guy's call data and investigate some of these guys who are in the address book," Vito told his partner John.

John nodded and got right at it. Schemes had left a trail big enough for a truck to drive through. The phone not only had his entire team's phone numbers stored in it, but there were hundreds of pictures in the phone of women and, even worse, all of his friends. The feds knew chances were that there were pictures and phone numbers of the others responsible for the Beneficial Bank job and possibly other robberies. A lot of phone numbers stored in the phone even had the pictures attached to them, making it easier for the feds to identify the owners of the numbers. It was only a matter of time before they narrowed it down.

At a little after ten o'clock, Ghost finally received the call he was waiting for. Hearing Kia's voice untied the knots in his stomach. Kia was let go by the abductors after they made sure the money was all there. Ghost picked her up from where they had let her go. She was given two quarters and told to call Ghost from a pay phone.

Guilt was eating Ghost up inside. Kia was distraught and had been quiet since she was back home. All she could think about was Khashan's dad and what he'd gone through when he was kidnapped. He was not as fortunate to be let loose.

They decided to let Kha stay with his uncle Bird. They didn't let him know what was going on. Ghost and Kia both weren't in any shape to take care of him now.

When Ghost picked Kia up, she was covered in what looked like dried-up vomit. Her hair was all over the place, and she smelled like she hadn't showered in days. She was only gone a little over twenty-four hours, but it looked and seemed like it had been much longer.

Though Kia was acting distant, she did allow Ghost to bathe her, and now the two of them were lying in the bed as one. Ghost cupped her in his arms and held her like he never wanted to lose her again. He was convinced, now more than ever, that he needed to leave the streets alone. But first he had to find and kill Reese.

"I love you, baby," he whispered in her ear.

Kia just nodded. Ghost started to tell her how he was going to kill the men responsible for her abduction, but he knew she wanted to forget about what had taken place, so he silently promised himself instead. He could only imagine what she was going through.

CHAPTER 28

After Shareef arrived in the city, the entire crew rounded up at a spot he owned. Over objections, Frog and Schemes met with the team to discuss getting at Reese and Mar. The two of them were like a toothache that kept coming back, and they wanted to get rid of them once and for all. Reese and Mar were almost impossible to find, so they needed to figure out a way to bring them out of their shell.

"Ghost, I know this may not be the best time, but I spoke with one of my investors, and he is looking into buying into some of the franchises we talked about," Shareef informed him.

Ghost just shook his head, but his silence indicated that now wasn't the time or place to discuss financial matters. There was still a bit of tension in the air about Schemes being left out on the truck job. Everyone felt the vibe, but no one wanted to speak on it. They needed to stay focused on the task at hand before Reese struck again.

"So, where are we gonna start looking to find these guys?" Schemes asked.

"Man, we've been tryna find them for months," Reem said. "It's no telling where they're at."

Ghost held his hand up to his chin while contemplating his next move. "Kia said she has no idea where she was at while they had her," Ghost said. "She said one of them did all the talking, but he was disguising his voice. But she said she's pretty sure it was Reese. But I spoke to him. It was him for sure."

"Well, we know who it was. The question is where we find him," Schemes said.

Silence pervaded the room. Finally, Shareef broke it by saying, "I have an idea."

"Let's hear it."

Shareef was the mastermind. He told them his plan while they all listened intently. Everyone had the *why-didn't-I-think-of-that* look on their faces once he shared what he was thinking.

The chase was about to end. The plan was sure to bring Reese to them.

Reese and Mar were riding down Broad Street together. They had just come from hitting it off with two women they met recently. Though they were at the chicks' house on the other side of town, they still were playing North Philly a lot. They had word of the money on their head, but that didn't stop them from getting some pussy.

They'd finally found a new hustle, and it was generating a nice piece of cash. Reese's mom, Lindell, sold everything from pills to liquor out of her house, so they supplied her with a large amount of pills, and she moved them like clockwork. Every few days or so, they would stop by the house to collect the money and give her more pills to sell. They were getting the prescription pills for dirt cheap, so they weren't too worried about Lindell messing up a little bit of the money, which she was good for.

"That chick you was fucking had a fat ass," Reese told Mar.

"I know, but Destiny is nice," Mar responded, referring to the one Reese was with. Mar was introduced to Tisha, who was Destiny's cousin.

"But that crib smelled like shit!" Reese said, and the two of them shared a laugh.

"Man, it seemed like the roaches were chilling with us," Mar said. "Every time I jumped at them, they didn't even move. They just looked at me like, 'What's up, nigga?'" Mar added, and they burst out laughing again.

Reese's phone rang. It was his mom calling.

"Reese, them damn boys just came here looking for you," Lindell told him. She sounded frantic.

"Who?" Reese asked, but knew the answer to his own question. He didn't think it would lead to this, but he knew he had already crossed the line and knew they would retaliate. He just didn't think they'd involve his mom in this. Lindell told him it was Ghost and his crew.

"Did they hurt you?"

"No, just come by here. I'm scared to death," Lindell emphasized.

"What did they say?"

"What do you think they said? They said they're going to kill you. What have you gotten yourself into, boy?"

"All right. Calm down, Mom, I'll be there, okay? What about the footballs and bananas? Do you still have them?" Reese asked, referring to the Percocet and Xanax he'd given her.

"Boy, these motherfuckers said they're going to kill your ass. They had guns, and here you are talking about some damn pills!" Lindell snapped. "You got me caught up in your bullshit, boy! They took everything!" she told him.

"Calm down, Mom. I'm on my way," Reese told her.

"Hurry up!" Lindell said before hanging the phone up.

Reese told Mar everything. They were heated. They knew it was on, but they couldn't believe Ghost had stooped low enough to involving his mom. He promised himself that he would kill Ghost and everyone who loved him. He was beating himself up about allowing his mom to be dragged into his drama.

A horn blared as Reese swerved between lanes on Broad Street and stepped on the gas.

"Mom!" Reese yelled as he walked in her house on Nelson Street. The lights in the house were off. The television was the only source of light, illuminating the living room. The house looked untouched. The usual beer bottles and Chinese food containers were scattered among other things.

Reese instantly got an eerie feeling, and, by the look on Mar's face, he could tell he felt the same. He couldn't believe it had come down to this. It was not enough room on earth for Ghost and Reese to exist together. Someone had to die, and Reese was determined for it to be Ghost. Reese and Mar pulled their burners out and crept through the house.

"Mom!" Reese called out again.

He was happy to hear Lindell answer after his second call. For a second, he thought she may have been dead.

"Boy, I'm up here!" Lindell's voice traveled from upstairs.

Reese started up the steps.

"You want me to stay down here?" Mar asked him, putting his gun back in his waistline.

"Naw, come on up, so we can see what happened," Reese told him, tucking his weapon as well.

The two of them ascended the steps and walked down the hallway to the rear bedroom. "Mom," Reese called out.

"I'm in here," she answered.

"Are you dressed? Mar is with me." "Yeah, come in," Lindell responded.

When Reese and Mar entered the room, they nearly shitted on themselves. Their reflexes weren't faster than the guns being pointed at their heads. Schemes and Frog were behind the bedroom door and had the drop on them as soon as they came in the room. Ghost and Reem stood next to Lindell, who was tied to a chair with a pitiful look her face. The game of cat and mouse was finally over. Now, it was do or die.

Ghost wore a devilish grin.

"What's wrong, Reese? You look like you've seen a *ghost*."

Reese thought he was dreaming. Well, at least, he hoped he was. But this was far from an illusion. It was a living nightmare. He, Mar, and his mom were all tied up to separate chairs. The three of them lost track of how long they'd been there.

Reese could tell it was still nighttime because it was still dark outside. He had been in and out of consciousness, so as far as he knew, it could have been the next night.

He started mumbling something, but it couldn't be made out because his mouth was gagged. He looked over and saw Mar staring at him. His mom was crying hysterically. He was out of it from the torture he had suffered from Ghost and the others. They had did it all from ripping off nails, cutting off fingers, to burning him with a hot iron. The pain was so excruciating he had passed out several times.

Reese was happy because it didn't look like his mom had had a finger laid on her. The three of them had shitted and urinated on themselves, so the room smelled terrible. If it weren't for anger, there would have been no way Ghost and his team would have been able to stand the smell.

Mar had dried blood on the side of his face that came from his temple. Though he was staring at Reese, he wasn't moaning and trying to get loose. As Reese looked closer, he noticed his man wasn't looking at him after all. He was looking past him. Mar's eyes had a blank look to them. Those of a dead man.

Reese started crying and shaking uncontrollably. Inside, he wasn't sure if he should be mad at his mom for leading him to Ghost or whether he should be guilty for having her dragged into this. He started saying something again, but it couldn't be made out.

Ghost untied the gag from his mouth. For some reason, Ghost was dragging out the inevitable. He wanted to return the pain to Reese that he felt when Kia was taken away from him.

"Please, man. Let her go. She has nothing to do with this," Reese cried.

Ghost smacked him so hard that blood flew out his mouth and splattered across Lindell's face. "She has everything to do with this!" Ghost snapped. He was gone. His temper was at full flare.

"Motherfucka, you took my wife from me!" Ghost continued. Reese tried to say something, but was smacked in the mouth again. "Shut up, pussy!"

Schemes and Reem were present, but it was as if they weren't. The two of them were standing still and allowing Ghost to get his shit off. Reem had tortured Reese for the attempted kidnapping of Toya, but he was ready to get it over with. Frog had left to complete a mission.

Ghost gagged Reese's mouth again. He didn't want to hear anything that he had to say. They all knew Reese was going to die.

"See, Reese, you made it this way. This never had to come down to this. You just couldn't let it go, huh?" Ghost said. "Let me tell you something, Reese. There are two types of war. There's one with rules and laws and another with none. The first is known to man; the other is known to beasts. Which one do you think I am?" Ghost asked before letting out a sinister laugh. "You took my wife from me," he continued. Reese started saying something again, but it couldn't be understood. There came another smack as Ghost said, "Now, I want my money back!"

"Call Frog," Ghost told Schemes. "It's time to get this piece-of-shit out of here."

Schemes dialed Frog's number and got him. Frog told him he was on his way back to the house. They sent Frog to get a stolen car, so they could finish things once and for all. Ghost wanted the quarter million back that he'd paid for the ransom.

The money was nothing compared to what he had, but it was the principle behind it. Reese had taken something from him, and he couldn't allow that. Schemes and Reem told him he was tripping. *Fuck the money*, was what they kept telling him, but Ghost insisted on getting back what was his.

Frog finally got back, and they untied Reese from the chair to take him outside to the car. They tied his hands and legs up and had his gun. Actually, they'd used Reese's gun to kill his man, Mar.

Reese squirmed and wiggled to get loose, but to no avail. Reese's mom cried uncontrollably as they dragged her son out the room. Ghost nodded at Frog as they left the room, and Frog stayed behind. A single gunshot echoed off the walls of the house. Lindell became a casualty of war.

Reese had taken them to his stash. He knew he was going to die, but was trying to delay it as long as possible. He never knew what could happen, so Reese was trying to stay alive as long as they let him.

Ghost was upset when Reese's stash came up a little shorter than a hundred grand. He wanted his entire two-fifty back, but he grew tired of the games with Reese.

Frog drove the car with Reese in the trunk while Reem, Ghost, and Schemes followed in another. Frog was reckless, and they used that to their advantage.

Together, they drove to Fairmount Park. They were lucky not to get stopped by the police because, at the time of night they were out, there weren't many other cars on the road. They pulled in the park and parked the cars out of sight. When Reese felt the car come to a stop, he started banging from inside the trunk. He was screaming, but with the gag on, and, inside the trunk, he was wasting his time. No one would hear him.

The smell of gasoline captivated Reese's nostrils. He knew he was in trouble once he smelled the gas. The worst way to die was drowning or being burned alive, and Reese was about to experience the latter.

The crew drowned the entire stolen car with gasoline. They emptied containers of it inside and outside the entire car. Besides Reese's screams and banging, there was nothing but crickets in the dark park.

"You do the honors." Reem handed Ghost a book of matches. They all looked at one another, and Schemes gave Ghost a nod before he struck the match and brought it to life. The flames lit up the night, and they all took a step back subconsciously to avoid the fire, which was ready to erupt.

Ghost threw the matches. It was as if the match moved in slow motion in the air. The car burst into flames, igniting the night. They stood there for a minute or two watching the car turn into ashes. It was like the weight of the world was being lifted off their shoulders with Reese and Mar gone.

The smell of burning flesh and metal foully polluted the air. Reese's cries grew louder and louder until they ceased. He banged on the trunk until the fire claimed his life. He was gone. Fried alive.

Tomorrow, he would be a star on *The First 48*.

THE TAKE

EPILOGUE

Once again, Reef was the mastermind behind things. Though he didn't get his hands dirty, he was the one who came up with the idea to finally get rid of Reese and Mar. The others didn't think it would work because Lindell was nothing more than a crack head, but Shareef knew better. He knew that using the mother would be the perfect rouse to drive him to them. Now, Reese was gone and Mar had gone with him. Lindell just happened to bear the wrong son. It had cost her life.

Shareef flew back to Miami. He was scheduled to meet with several investors to set things up for Ghost and Reem to purchase some franchises. The old timer was filthy rich, but, before he left, he was already telling Ghost about another big job he had lined up. Ghost looked at him like he was crazy when he mentioned the job. Ghost insisted that he was done with the game. But taking money wasn't anything like selling drugs. For some reason, it wasn't as easy for Ghost to give it up. Maybe it was the adrenaline rush and the fast money.

"So, baby, how is the wedding planning coming along?" Ghost asked Kia, as he entered the room.

"Great! You're going to love it."

Kia was looking at magazines and catalogs for wedding planning. The bed was scattered with various catalogs. Ghost shoved some to the side and laid behind his fiancée, who was sitting on the edge of the bed. After wrapping his arms around her waist, he took a deep whiff of her body spray and blew on the side of her stomach, drawing a giggle from Kia.

"How is my little man in there?" Ghost rubbed her stomach. "I love you, baby. I can't wait to marry you."

"I know, baby. I love you, too. You're so good to me."

Ghost had convinced Shareef to let them get married in his mansion. It wasn't hard to persuade him to allow them to fly down and get married in his home. He really liked Ghost. He was his friend's son. Together, they had visited Khalil, Ghost's father. It was strained at first, but Ghost broke in, and they enjoyed the visit. They promised to help Khalil once he was released, but under one condition: as long as he stopped getting high. Khalil promised he would leave the crack alone for good and get his life together. The visit was the best thing that had happened to him while he was down. Not only did he get to rekindle the relationship with his son and longtime friend, but he, also, had something to look forward to—the take. He was set for the remainder of the bid because they dropped a few grand on his commissary account before they left.

Ghost gave Kia a hundred-thousand dollar budget for the wedding. She couldn't believe her man had become a millionaire. And stayed alive while doing it at that. The hundred grand would go a long way because they didn't need to rent anywhere out since they already had an extravagant place to hold the ceremony.

Ghost collected the bounty money that was out on Reese and Mar's head for the counterfeit money. All together it was one hundred and fifty thousand out on Reese's head, but, once the job was done, Ghost had gotten rid of Reese. Suave gave him the fifty grand plus an extra twenty-five thousand and a brick of coke as well. They loved the way Reese was taken out. They begged Ghost for the details, but he wouldn't give any. It was his pleasure to get rid of the two men who had caused so much havoc in his life, but he still collected the bounty for the hell of it.

He gave Kia a hundred grand of the money for the wedding and let the others split the rest. Reem took twenty-five grand, and Frog and Schemes took the same, but the two of them kept the brick of coke as well. Ghost wanted nothing to do with the drugs.

Generously, Ghost let Frog keep the money that they got from Reese's stash, which was close to a hundred grand. Though Reem had put up some ransom money for Kia, he didn't mind letting Frog keep what was retrieved. He needed the money more than the rest of them, and he had put in a lot of work, so it was only right. Schemes was the only one who objected to the stash money being given to Frog. He wanted some, too. He was greedy, but they didn't give him any of the money. Frog had earned it.

"Look, baby." Kia pointed at something in the catalog. "That's nice," Ghost said, with only a glimpse at what she was pointing to.

"You didn't even look, Kevin!" She playfully hit him.

"Because I'm too busy looking at you," Ghost told her.

He grabbed her and pulled her into the clutches of his arms. He started kissing her passionately, and she invited his move. Buried under his body, she looked into his eyes. She was in love. They had everything. Money, cars, home, and, soon, they would have a child together. But none of it meant anything to her without him. He was all she wanted.

"Baby," she whispered. "Please don't leave me. Promise me again you're done for good."

"I promise," he told her almost sincerely.

Then, he thought about the job Shareef told him he was working on. He tried to shake the thought, but the truth was he loved the take.

Agents Boselli and Graham were stationed outside the address they believed Schemes was hiding out at. They used the phone records to track down the entire crew, and, with some expert FBI work, they found who they were looking for.

"Do you think he's in there?" Vito asked.

"According to our surveillance team, they say he's in there right now. He was seen going inside not long ago with a duffel bag in his hand."

"Oh, yeah?" Vito came alive. "I'd bet I know what's in the bag."

"If I was a betting man, I'd bet with you, not against you."

"Was he alone when he went in?" Vito was ready to make a move.

"Yeah, according to them he was.""All right. Let's go see if we can find out what's in that bag." The two of them emerged from the car and crossed the street, heading toward the house. Schemes was in for a rude awakening. They climbed the steps cautiously before approaching the door. Vito put his ear to the door to see if he could hear any activity inside while John, the taller of the two, took a peek in the window.

"Can you see anything?"

"Nah, nothing."

"I can hear someone. Sounds like they're arguing about something."

"Well, let's join the party," John said.

Schemes and Frog went inside a house he had rented under an alias. He knew he was wanted by the feds for, at least, questioning. His lawyer told him the feds wanted to see him for questioning and DNA samples. There was no way Schemes was going to allow that.

"Ghost really looked out for me with that paper. I needed that." Frog was as happy as ever. Ghost had broken him off with the money from the stash they took from Reese, and then with some of the ransom that was on Reese's head and a brick of coke. Schemes got a brick of coke as well and set up a sell to a buyer who had just brought the two bricks.

Schemes had just completed the transaction and returned to the house where Frog was waiting for him. He had no idea that he was being trailed by the feds the entire time. Even worse, they were outside his door right now.

Schemes dumped the contents of the bag on the kitchen table. He had sold the kilos for a small twenty-five thousand a piece.

"Come on and count this shit up so we can split it up," Frog said, taking a seat at the table.

"Man, I got rid of the work. We ain't splitting this. I'll give you fifteen of it," Schemes said. He was still upset about Ghost giving Frog the money from Reese's stash.

"What?" Frog jumped up from the table.

"You heard me! You didn't give me none of the money from Reese's stash."

"Are you serious?" Frog couldn't believe his ears. This was his flesh and blood on the other side of the table and here he was being greedy. Frog had been nothing but loyal to his cousin, and this was how he was being repaid.

"Hell, yeah! I'm serious! I put my ass on the line to sell that work, so it's only right I get more."

Frog lost it. He smacked the money from the table, sending it flying around the kitchen. "Fuck this money! I'll take all of this shit!" He pulled his gun from his waist and pointed it at Schemes.

A sly grin eased on Schemes's face. "After all we have been through, this is what it comes down to?"

"Yeah, this is how it is! You're a fucking snake, cuz!" Frog grimaced through clenched teeth.

"I'm a snake? I put you on money! Me!" Schemes patted his chest.

"I put work in, too! Don't forget that!"

There was a knock at the door, but they were so caught up in the moment that they ignored it.

"Yeah, you're right, Frog. You're a rider! You definitely put that work in, but don't forget I put this shit together for us. That quarter million we got in there is *me*! I put that together. My idea!" Schemes said.

Another knock.

Schemes looked toward the door in the front room.

"Now, get that gun outta my face!"

Frog didn't budge. He kept the gun pointed at Schemes's face. He kept his finger on the trigger, and, with the slightest amount of pressure, Schemes would be joining Smitty. Frog knew his cousin had a point. Schemes was responsible for putting together the plan to kidnap Kia, from which they came up with the quarter million. The paper that they got from Reese's stash and the bounty money weren't part of the plan; that was just icing on the cake. Ghost and everyone else were really convinced that Reese was behind the abduction. It was the perfect plan, and Schemes took pride in being the mastermind behind it all.

Frog knew Schemes was a problem, and his instincts told him to pull the trigger. He was a monster that needed to be killed.

Another knock.

Louder.

"FBI! Open the door! Donald, we know you are in there. We just want to ask you a few questions," one of the agents shouted from the other side of the door.

The sound of the FBI made Frog and Schemes's hearts sink. "Looks like we have some company," Schemes said, happier than ever to hear the presence of the feds. He was anti-police. He hated them. But, right now, the knock at the door was like music to his ears. It might save his life.

Frog's mind went blank. The feds were at the door. He felt like he was going to go to jail for a long time anyway, so how much could it hurt to get rid of Schemes? His mind was playing tricks on him, and he was on the verge of blacking out.

"So, what are you going to do? It looks like we have some company," Schemes said with a sadistic smirk on his face. He showed no emotion, but, on the inside, he was scared to death because he knew Frog was a killer.

Frog gritted his teeth and tightened his grip on the gun as he listened to the thoughts in his head: *You can never trust a nigga named Schemes*.